I0552167

Published by Gracie Dancer LLC
www.rldonovan.com

Printed in the United States of America

Cover Design by Bozell
Cover Photography Copyright © by MinorWhite Studios

ISBN (eBook Edition): 978-1-943976-05-8
ISBN (Print Edition): 978-1-943976-04-1

First Edition

ACKNOWLEDGEMENTS

My husband, Joe, for everything he does that makes my life better in a million ways. To my mom, Gloria, for being you and showing me that a woman can be awesome – and mean.

The incredible Bozell crew: Heather McCain for cover design, Kerrey Lubbe for editing and Sheryl Ann Hayes for formatting.

My friend, Rosemary Duhaime for proofing.

Ed Almsteier for his technical expertise on the wine industry.

Scott Drickey for cover photography.

IN MEMORY

Of my Leemann, Janssen, Walgering and Leveroni relatives for making me who I am. And of my Mother-in-law, Marie Nole Donovan and my Step-father, James Knak for contributing to my belief in myself.

[CHAPTER 1]

The alarm went off early this morning. 6:15 could be painful, and today it was. Then I remembered my 9:30 meeting with Ed and it made me smile. For about a year now, Ed has been a client of Marcel, the Omaha ad agency that I, Donna Leigh, have owned with my business partner, Liv, for over a decade.

Ed Von Hapsburg was a friend turned client. His background was in the food and beverage industry. Ed was unique in that he had equal experience in both. He started out as a restaurant and catering chef with a specialty in desserts that could make a grown woman cry. After years on his feet, those sturdy but flawed tootsies gave him an ultimatum and he was forced to choose a profession with more butt time than foot time. So he went to work for a wine distributor.

Ed made it a point to learn everything there was to know about growing grapes, blending wine and distributing a top quality end product. When the inevitable moment came that he outgrew his employer, Ed raised enough capital to become a winemaker himself. These days he spent time between his Sonoma winery on the west coast and his Omaha based distribution facility. It worked out well since Ed and his wife, Eva, had been Omaha residents for their entire 30-year marriage and his daughter, Abby, lived on the coast with her husband and new baby. Abby ran the winery while Ed ran distribution. Eva had recently left her lucrative corporate IT position to manage the website and Social Media for the family business.

In the little over a year that Ed and his family had taken control of a small vineyard, whose family-owned management team had dwindled to an old and infirm single member, so much had happened. With his keen instincts regarding all things wine related, Ed and his investors (of which my husband Jon and I were a very modest part) and the marketing expertise of Marcel, Ed's brand, Bohóc, named for the small Hungarian village where his mother was born, had become more renowned than we could have expected. Discerning wine aficionados were lining up to buy cases.

After a quick breakfast and a luke-warm shower – I love a steamy shower but the massive menopausal post-shower hot flash that always follows forces a cooler head and temperature to prevail – I left for the office and my meeting with Ed. Besides, arriving with the tell-tale menopausal sweat mustache would give Ed way too much ammo to turn our meeting into a three-ring circus with me as the featured clown. He never missed a chance to take a shot.

Since moving to the MidWest, Ed was one of the few true smart-asses I got to hang out with regularly. MidWesterners are so perky and friendly; nothing like the dark, brooding and moody narcissists so typical of the east coast. Finding that charming and upbeat individual in the northeast was like finding a needle in a haystack. Problem was, you got used to the snarky smart-asses that surrounded you, and then when you moved out to big sky country, it was an adjustment. Hanging out with Ed was like taking a trip back home to the fast paced world where there was always someone jumping on every little thing that came out of your mouth.

The meeting was set up in our medium-sized conference room, Captain Jack. There was coffee and tea, water and soda, fruit and pastries. Today, Ed wanted to talk about a new sparkling wine he'd had in the planning for a while now. We would have to conduct research to confirm the target audience interest and he'd need a logo and label design as well as all of the accompanying promotional materials. It was another big assignment. At this rate, Bohóc was shaping up to be one of our larger clients.

Ed's appearance invigorated the entire staff. He walked in to a cacophony of sounds from catcalls to whistles. Not only was he a growing client on the Marcel roster, he was also a huge favorite of the crew. Ed was fun in a way only a true smart-ass can be. He made everyone laugh, but he also knew when to allow himself the vulnerability of admitting when he wasn't always an expert on everything. In other words, he left the marketing to the marketers and he stuck to the wine business, which is what he knew.

Today Ed had dressed his 6 foot 2 frame in his typical light colored oxford shirt, tan Dockers and his sockless feet were clad in light brown moccasins. His head had sported bowl-cut brown hair and a 70's porn star mustache for as long as I'd known him. Startlingly blue eyes were framed by Ed's modest wire rimmed glasses. I sat across from him in my typical all-black all the time business wardrobe (in truth it was my round the clock wardrobe, business, leisure and sleep all took place in all black – inside and out).

After our typical verbal banter – I think he said something about my only needing a long black wig to pass for Elvira – I don't know, I wasn't really listening – until we got down to business. Our new Chief Marketing Officer, Maxie, wanted a debriefing from Ed on his desired target audience. Maxie Morgan was a hard charging, razor sharp, take no prisoners kind of girl and she wanted proof that Ed and his wine empire were as impressive as we'd described. Under her expert direction, we'd be conducting both qualitative and quantitative research, so our data analytics guy, Craig, was gathering the information he needed to pin down the list for the online survey.

Once we made the shift it was all business. The staffers that had not previously met with Ed, including Maxie, soon became aware that he was a very savvy businessman – and not just a jovial pal of mine. Seeing the shift in the look on their faces was so interesting; I couldn't help but feel pride in my friend. He knew his stuff and that was a fact.

By the time we'd finished our meeting it was getting close to lunchtime. Ed decided to call his wife, Eva, to see if the three of us could grab a quick lunch in the old market. I knew that Jon, my husband, was busy trying to close a deal so I didn't bother to check to see if he could join us.

Eva thought she could break free for a quick bite, so we agreed to meet her at the Jackson St. Tavern which was within walking distance from the Marcel offices. Jackson St. had good food and a comfortable ambiance. This was a bit out of character for Ed. Normally he would insist we find a new and adventurous dining experience, some new and unique type of meal venue – something being touted by the reliable foodies. But time was against us this time. Within minutes of being seated, the owner came out and made a big fuss over Ed. I sat back and watched him handle his newfound celebrity with grace. By the time they'd covered all the news in the food and wine arena, Eva had arrived. I greeted her with a continental double cheek buss and we seated ourselves to take a serious look at the menu.

Mid-way through the meal, Ed's phone rang. With an exasperated eye-roll he stood, simultaneously gesturing his intention of taking this call elsewhere so Eva and I could continue enjoying our meal while he dealt with his challenge. Once Ed was safely out of view, Eva's whole demeanor shifted dramatically; she instantly went from serene to visibly agitated.

"Donna, I'm so glad we have time to talk alone," she

whispered, "I've been hoping we'd get a moment."

"What's troubling you, Eva?" I asked, not at all sure I'd want to hear the answer.

"I'm so worried about Ed. He hasn't been himself lately; we had our two best months since we started the business, and when we realized it – he just shrugged."

"It's true, that doesn't sound like Ed," I offered, "but maybe he's afraid if he gets too excited he'll jinx everything."

"There's more," Eva was quick to chime in. "The other day I walked into his office to ask him a question, and I caught him looking very pensive. He tried to hide the email he'd been reading, but I caught enough of a glimpse to realize that someone had threatened him. He was quick to cover it up; I'm sure he didn't want to worry me needlessly, but I just know the threat is connected to his strange behavior – I knew it instantly."

"Did you question him about the email?"

"No, his effort to keep me in the dark was so obvious I was afraid to call him on it at the risk of stressing him out even further. You know after all these years of marriage, you can tell when to dive in and when to back off the diving board."

I nodded. When you've been married for over thirty years, there is a telepathic connection that makes verbal communication almost unnecessary. Sometimes we rely on the telepathy to such an extent that we don't communicate verbally even when it's essential. How many times have we had that conversation "you remember when I told you..."

"No, I have no idea what you're talking about." I would venture to say that most of the disagreements these days were centered on the fact that one of us swore to have informed the other of something while the other swore to be totally ignorant. Who was usually right? Who knows?

"How can I help?" I asked.

"I honestly don't know, Donna, what do you think?" she asked with a slight note of pleading in her voice.

Before I had a chance to respond, Ed was back from his call.

"Alright, what are you two conspiring about?" Ed asked. And did I detect a hint of genuine suspicion in his question? Apparently Ed's telepathy was also in high gear. I put money on the fact that Ed knew Eva was worried about him and he was working hard to put her mind at ease. Oh Ed, you're so naïve!

"Wouldn't you like to know," I chimed in. I figured that the more I could help put both of them at ease, the more valuable my contribution would be. Okay, so I'm no less naïve than Ed!

Eva rapidly changed the subject and we finished our meal rather quickly. On our way out of the restaurant, Eva gave me a "call me if you think of something" look that couldn't have been clearer if she'd shouted it directly into my ear.

Who knows, maybe telepathy was more a product of age than sharing a long term relationship – maybe both.

Back in the office, I gave some thought to Ed and his

circumstances. He was a guy who wasn't afraid to call it like it was; his up front style had certainly pissed some people off in his day – but enough to want to harm him? That seemed extreme for the rather mild irritation he tended to cause people. Unless, of course, some serious business issues had arisen unbeknownst to me. It might make sense to make a list of the various areas related to Ed's business where something potentially serious might have been likely to surface.

The first possibility that came to mind was his purchase of the vineyard. Might there have been another party who had coveted the vineyard only to lose it to Ed and his family? That seemed like a serious enough area. Or perhaps his wine distributorship had caused a competitive distributor to lose a sizeable chunk of business; that would be another issue not to be taken lightly. I immediately dismissed the possibility of a friend or relative feeling as though Ed had bested them and left them bitter and envious of his success.

With my list finished I made a few phone calls and answered a few emails. I wanted to call Eva before she left for home so that she'd be free to talk about her concerns, so I put in a call before my 3 o'clock meeting. Unfortunately, Eva was not at her desk, so I left a quick message and gathered my files before heading over to the conference room.

By the time the meeting ended, Eva had called back and left a voicemail for me.

"Sorry to get you all anxious about Ed," she started, "I'm letting this get to me too much. I want to just try to forget the whole thing for now. I know Ed will tell me if there's something to worry about. Until then I'm going to focus on my main priorities, and let him handle his own business. Thanks for listening, though. It's comforting to know you're there, in case."

Poor Eva, she was trying so hard to ignore her instincts because she wanted to believe Ed was in no danger. How many times had I done that myself? Over the years, I've come to learn that ignoring my instincts always causes bigger problems later on – but would I be doing the same thing in Eva's place? Most likely. It's so much easier to be sure of what do to when it's not you and your family involved. I wouldn't criticize Eva for trying to convince herself there wasn't a problem, but I wasn't about to ignore her angst. Eva generally had flawless instincts so I suspected things would get worse before getting better. I wasn't sure what good I could do without directly involving Eva, but I would certainly give it a try for both their sakes.

[CHAPTER 2]

At home that night I shared my concerns with Jon. He and my three bulldogs listened carefully as I outlined our lunch and Eva's concerns over Ed. Before Jon had a chance to weigh in on the whole situation, Jasmine, a determined bulldog with a beautiful red coat, a pure snow white head and one brown and one blue eye, signaled that she wanted food... now. She walked over to the dog closet in the corner of the kitchen, reached in and grabbed the corner of the 40 lb. food bag to give it a yank. Then she circled back to where Jon and I were sitting with Roxi, our outspoken cream and brown spotted sweetheart and Sadie, our eager to please strawberry blonde puppy, to drive home her point.

After a brief puppy parade through the kitchen, things finally settled down.

Jon felt that, as long as the bulldogs were eating, we might as well enjoy our own dinner as well, so we took our wine glasses over to the kitchen counter and finished preparing our own meal. Once we were able to sit down and eat, I asked Jon if he had any thoughts about our earlier conversation. He shook his head "no."

"Not yet, I need to give it a little more thought," he offered between mouthfuls of his turkey burger.

I nodded my acceptance. Jon was never quick to come to a conclusion. His analytical style was thorough and exacting – and he virtually always came to the right conclusion. Unfortunately, he'd recently exhibited pinpoint accuracy regarding the murder of some people I'd known through business. In each of those cases he'd been the first one to identify the murderer. I suppressed a shudder when I thought that there had been an inordinately high number of murders in our personal acquaintance set. Apparently two recently murdered acquaintances were enough to make me paranoid beyond reason, and I clung to the hope that Eva's instincts were flawed and Ed couldn't possibly be in real danger. Now it was my turn to rationalize – but I just couldn't face the fact that something might happen to my friend.

As we finished our main course, sipping the last few drops of wine, we began to devise a game plan for helping Eva think this problem through. Jon agreed that Ed would be cagey about a direct threat in order to protect his family. He would do anything to keep them from worrying. We thought Eva might do well to call our mutual friend, Olivier, owner of the regionally famous French restaurant, Le Voltaire. Ed and Olivier had worked together for a number of years and they were very close friends. It was far more likely that Ed would have confided something concerning to Olivier.

* * *

"Let me know what you find out, Eva," I pushed.

"Oh absolutely, I would never leave you hanging," Eva assured me.

She also assured me she would swing by Olivier's restaurant the next day and meet him for lunch. As soon as I shared my suggestion Eva realized that was her best means of getting to the bottom of the whole thing without unduly concerning Ed. It's kind of weird; sometimes the most obvious solution evades us when we're all caught up in a difficult dilemma. I was sure that talking to Olivier would go a long way toward making Eva feel better.

With the worries of the day addressed, I was ready to hit the sheets in preparation of tomorrow's crazy schedule.

[CHAPTER 3]

After a morning of debriefing the team for a huge research project, we shared a quick lunch and dashed back for a 1:15 meeting.

The meeting ran long and by the time I got back to my desk it was 4:30 and the message light was flashing. A quick check confirmed that Eva was among the callers. She had an update for me and requested I call her after dinner that night. Shoot, now I was really curious. Oh well, I guess a few more hours wouldn't kill me!

Once home, Jon had prepared a Cooking Light feast. It never ceased to amaze me that he could flip through a magazine, see something that piqued his curiosity and turn it into a gourmet delight in the blink of an eye. The smells emanating from the kitchen were incredible! I couldn't wait to dig into this latest spread. Naturally, Jon selected the perfect complimentary wine – served in Riedel glasses to maximize the experience. Once sated from food and wine, I was ready to settle in and watch a new murder mystery on Netflix. The flick would have to wait, however, while I phoned Eva to find out about her lunch with Olivier.

She answered the phone with a weariness that broke

my heart.

"God Eva, I'm really sorry," I offered, "sounds like my brilliant idea made you feel worse instead of better."

"No, Donna, your advice was great," she assured me in a voice rife with concern, "it's not your fault that the more I know, the more concerned I get."

That didn't go a long way toward making me feel better. I always pride myself on helping friends and colleagues by encouraging them to talk and think through their troubles. So often they find that their worries have been blown out of proportion along with their sense of lacking control. That didn't appear to be the case this time. It seemed as though Eva wasn't the only one with grave concerns for Ed.

"Donna, I've never seen Olivier this nervous. He tried so hard to put me at ease, but I've known him for far too long."

During their lunch, Olivier had opened up to Eva and shared his concern about Ed. He too was worried that Ed was being threatened, he had observed that Ed was seriously troubled. On the positive side, Eva and Olivier had decided to confront Ed together. They felt their joint support might serve to put him enough at ease to let his hair down (meta-phorically, of course, Ed's longest hair was on his mustache) and share his worries with them. Maybe together they could devise a strategy that would get Ed out from under his troubles, whatever they were.

I acknowledged my agreement with their game plan and bid my good-byes to Eva. Getting off the phone I felt more concerned than ever. Damn, I had so hoped that Eva's lunch with Olivier would prove her concerns to be groundless and our worries over Ed could be put to rest once and for all. I should have known. How often, in life, do things work out so easily?

Eva and Olivier had set their lunch with Ed for the following Wednesday. I thought that was probably the best place to start, but I had given Eva some thoughts on what to look for in Ed's behavior and mannerisms so that if things escalated to a point where he was really running scared, she'd know not to wait to confront him. Hopefully with enough knowledge she'd have the confidence to wait until the lunch with Ed and Olivier. I felt that I'd done everything I could to protect Ed and placate Eva until they could get him to open up about his concerns.

Sadly, I could not have been more wrong.

At about mid-morning the next day I received a Skype from Jon. I'm in the vicinity and I need to stop by and talk for a minute. Hmmm, that was odd; I can't recall Jon ever doing that. Before I had a chance to overthink his message, Jon arrived at Marcel.

The second I saw his face I knew something terrible had happened. Just seeing him made me start to hyperventilate. Jon coaxed me into the nearest conference room.

"Donna," he began tentatively, "there's been a tragic accident. Ed is dead."

"Ed who?" I asked before panic and horror sunk in, "what

kind of accident?"

"Ed was on his way home last night and the brakes in his car failed as he rounded a particularly lethal turn in the road," Jon explained, "at least they say he never knew what hit him."

"This is Ed we're talking about? Eva's Ed?" I pushed.

"Yes Donna, Ed," Jon confirmed with a catch in his throat.

I can't honestly say I remember the rest of the morning. I do know that when I was finally able to eat a bite of food I was at home and the sun was beginning to set. As I sat at the kitchen counter, numbly munching on some almond crackers, I couldn't be sure if my car was in our garage, or back in the office parking lot. I would have guessed the latter considering I was in absolutely no shape to drive.

A quick glance as I walked past a mirror revealed that I'd had at least one good healthy cry. And there was a whole lot to cry about. The thought dawned on me that if I was having this reaction to the tragic news, how must Eva be feeling? We needed to find out if there was anything we could do for her.

I found Jon downstairs at the desk in his home office. An unconventional home office that featured a smoky glass desk, some oak file cabinets on wheels that slid neatly under the desk, a red pot belly stove and a bunch of Yankee Stadium photos from the early 1900's to now. Across the room was a wall of built in oak cabinetry, and fitted perfectly between the cabinet to ceiling bookcases was a 70-inch TV. A comfortable, taupe overstuffed couch and oversized chair in washable suede flanked Jon's "office area" and provided seating for TV viewers. During the day when Jon worked at his desk, the couch and chair were the ideal napping places for three sleepy bulldogs.

Without benefit of a clear head, I tentatively questioned Jon as to the source of his information and whether or not he knew what was happening with Eva. Apparently Olivier had been contacted by the authorities and asked to help Eva in the first few hours of her ordeal. According to Olivier, Eva was in complete shock and wasn't even able to shed a tear at this point.

In his concern for Eva, along with his certainty that I would force him to call back for details, had they been lacking, for once Jon had managed to get every bit of information. Eva would be staying with Olivier and Desiree until her daughter and son-in-law were able to fly out to help her with funeral arrangements.

Wow, it was so hard to think of Eva having to make funeral arrangements for Ed. A little further pressing revealed that Olivier would let us know the moment he felt that Eva was up to talking or visiting with friends. I certainly had no reason to be concerned that she'd get fed – living with Olivier, the chef/owner of Le Voltaire restaurant would ensure that Eva would not be lacking for sustenance, although she may not choose to avail herself of any culinary pleasures in her time of grief.

About an hour later the phone rang. It was Olivier, asking

if Jon and I would pick Eva's daughter and son-in-law up at the airport and drop them off at Ed and Eva's home at around noon the next day. Naturally we were eager to pitch in and help Eva and her family. I was pretty sure I'd be working from home the next day anyway. Neither Jon nor I were functioning at anywhere near full capacity, so we agreed that double teaming on tasks in the near term would substantially increase the odds of desired results.

After dropping Abby and her husband William off at Ed and Eva's, both Jon and I were feeling a renewed surge of sadness over Ed's tragic accident. We offered to take his daughter and son-in-law to lunch, but neither had any appetite. Luckily we had stopped at the supermarket on our way to the airport to pick up a few necessities that would keep them going if their lethargy and disinterest in food kept them from even caring about the basics. We knew that with the arrival of her family, Olivier was returning Eva back to her home. As much as we wanted to express our sorrow and support, we did not want to be voyeurs in such a sorrowful family reunion. Eva knew how we felt about Ed and how we'd do anything to help her through all of this.

We stopped in mid-town for a quick bite before going back home to finish up some work. As we were finishing lunch at a nondescript place with nondescript food – one that we'd not likely return to any time soon, Jon's phone rang. It was Olivier, telling Jon that it might be a good idea for us to stop by and visit Eva after dinner that evening. He also said the memorial service for Ed would be held in two days. Jon volunteered to make a few dishes for the luncheon at Eva's after the service.

That was one great thing about the friends we'd made since moving to Omaha a decade earlier; the support through a difficult time was unparalleled.

[CHAPTER 4]

The next day at the office, everyone was extremely solic-itous and the few that had worked directly with Ed were noticeably depressed. It was amazing to see the impact a tragic accident like this can create throughout a community, much less Ed's circle of intimates.

Seeing Geanna, our head of research, looking so desolate brought to mind our visit with Ed's daughter Abby the previous night. It was impressive to see her raw courage. As subdued as she was it stunned me when she actually started to console me during a momentary display of grief that slipped out when she was telling me the details of the accident and how she had learned of the tragedy. That kind of strength was always inspiring to witness. For a moment, I even thought I glimpsed a flash of guilt at my sadness. It just blew my mind completely. She was truly an amazing woman. I knew that Jon had been equally moved, but he put the bulk of his energy into maintaining his stoicism; and he cleared his throat a lot. I noticed that was a male technique to keep from breaking down during these unbearably diffi-cult times of emotional up-heaval. Losing Ed in a senseless accident was unfathomable.

Bringing myself back to the present I resolved to push those thoughts into the back of my mind or risk a messy breakdown in the office. It didn't help that everyone around me was so concerned for my benefit, and sad about Ed themselves. The day was a cornucopia of sadness and sorrow. It was impossible to escape. I thought Ed would be touched to realize the major impact his loss would have on so many people.

It's just not something the average person spends a lot of time thinking about; and if it had come up while he was alive, no doubt I would have assured him that we'd have to pay strangers to get a decent crowd at his funeral; let's face it, I rarely missed an opportunity to take a shot at Ed. The realization was sobering, there was never a time when we'd genuinely conveyed to Ed how much we cared about him and how important he was as a friend. I was truly sorry he hadn't known the extent to which we cared. Although it was too late to rectify the situation with Ed, I hoped this tragedy would teach us a valuable lesson about communicating our feelings for each other. Or maybe it was just the hormones talking – menopausal women are prone to momentary lapses into melancholy and deep thought. We don't always need the death of a close friend to bring on an attack of paralyzing thoughtfulness. There are so many things about menopause that are inconvenient; making you think is just one example.

At about mid-morning my phone rang. It was Jules La Plage, another friend from our gourmet feasts and wine tasting group at Le Voltaire; the group through which we had met Ed and Eva in the first place. After a few minutes of acknowledging the sadness we both felt, Jules became uncharacteristically quiet. Then he cleared his throat; yep, that was a male thing alright. He began again, but slowly, and so softly that I actually had difficulty hearing him.

"Donna, what do you think?" he started.

"What do I think about what, Jules?" I asked. It was not like Jules to beat around the bush. He was a man who typically got right to the point; that was one of the things I liked best about him.

"Ed," he continued giving me very little more in the way of information.

"Hey Jules," I pushed, "just say it!"

"Donna, do you think it was an accident?"

Oh god! Clearly I hadn't been thinking. Was it an accident? My mind raced through the details. How did it not occur to me that murder had to be considered before it could be ruled out? I took a moment to compose my thoughts before responding to Jules. It had not even occurred to me, not once.

"Now that I think of it, no, probably not."

"So what will you do?" he asked.

"What do you mean, what will I do?"

"You know, to start the investigation," Jules finished.

I was stuck in neutral. Still a little shocked that such an obvious possibility had never occurred to me and still a lot in shock that Ed may have been murdered. And now, Jules was clearly expecting me to take the lead in conducting an investigation, or at least in convincing the police to conduct an investigation. But this was so different. Sure, I had been involved in two murder investigations fairly recently; and the victims had been women I'd known. But this was completely different. Ed was my friend and my first priority would be to protect his wife Eva and his daughter Abby. I couldn't imagine proactively pushing for an investigation that would so obviously cause them untold pain with no chance of bringing Ed back. I didn't see how I could even conceive of such a thing.

"Hey Donna," Jules was evidently not going to give up on this notion easily.

"Jules," I started.

"Donna, I just want you to know that you can count on me. I mean I will jump in and help you out in any way I can," he concluded.

"Look, Jules," I chimed in again.

"What have you done so far?" he naturally wanted to know.

Oh man, where would I start? I had to explain to Jules that he was way ahead of me and I couldn't even begin to formulate a game plan until I'd had a chance to absorb his theory. I did manage to caution him on the importance of handling things with the utmost discretion until we knew for sure what we were dealing with. I emphasized the need to keep Eva and Abby in the dark until we had more information. There was no way I would let them get hurt unnecessarily.

Jules agreed completely. As upset as he was about losing Ed, I could have sworn that he was equally as excited about the chance to work on a murder investigation with me. The more I thought about it, the more I thought that Jules was probably right about Ed being murdered; but the more I thought about it, the less excited I was about the prospect of conducting a murder investigation for someone I really liked and whose wife was a very close friend.

Jules and I hung up with the understanding that we would both think things over and make a list of the details that could support our hypothesis. I agreed that I would also create a preliminary game plan so we could begin the actual investigation before too long had passed. Jules reminded me that the first twenty-four hours after a murder were the most critical in terms of finding evidence – and we had already long passed that deadline.

After hanging up the phone I found myself in somewhat of a daze. Unable to focus on any of the tasks at hand, I decided that when I felt a bit more like myself, I would drive home for lunch. I really needed a bit of a break, and I was sure a conversation with Jon would be helpful. I was still very unclear as to how I could remove my own emotions enough to be able to lend anything worthwhile to the investigation. Up until now I had taken pride in my tough reputation – whether real or perceived. But this was a game changer; I could already feel that I was anything but tough, and that would hurt me if I concluded that Ed had been murdered and I was committed to finding his killer.

[CHAPTER 5]

I sat at my kitchen counter eating sliced turkey on diet wheat bread as Jon stood nearby drinking his protein drink. My kitchen wasn't super modern, but it featured beautiful oak cabinets and a granite countertop that was mostly black with an inflection of reddish-brown stone coordinating perfectly with the finish of the cabinets. It glinted beautifully in the light. Appliances were stainless steel with a black gas cooktop and lighting was also stainless and leaning toward ultra-modern. The backsplash was a vanilla wall tile with coordinating glass tile along the bottom as it met the counter.

I loved my kitchen. It was the perfect blend of reuse/green and chic modern; and it was a comfortable place to be.

"Yeah, I figured that possibility would surface sooner rather than later," he responded to my recap of this morning's phone call with Jules.

Figures. Was I the last person to consider that Ed's accident was no accident? Was everyone else ahead of me?

"When did that occur to you, Jon? And were you planning on saying anything?" I grilled him as delicately as I could manage while feeling decidedly dullwitted – at least compared to everyone else I knew.

"I'd have to say immediately," he responded nonplussed.

Clearly Jon had not caught an edge of any kind in my voice; I suppose that was good since it wasn't my intention to antagonize him.

"Like, immediately after you heard about Ed's accident?" I pushed, because that's what I do.

"Pretty much," he looked up, now curious as to my need for this much information and detail.

I could see by the look in his eyes that it had dawned on him I was being a tad petulant.

"God, Donna, you were in shock from learning you'd just lost a friend – you shouldn't beat yourself up that the prospect of murder didn't immediately jump into your mind," he consoled and reprimanded at the same time.

"I guess," I acceded. Still not feeling like the super-sleuth that my reputation suggested, "so do you know who did it?"

"I have some thoughts, but nothing solid yet."

I hadn't expected that. I only asked him that question to make him feel dumb – at least as dumb as I was feeling. I mean, Jon was good, but even I didn't think he was THAT good. In the last two murders, as in every murder mystery movie we've ever seen together, and most novels about murder, Jon could figure out the killer – sometimes before the murder had occurred. As proud as I was of Jon's deductive ability – it could be annoying at times.

Jon shot me his "listen to yourself" look. After so many years of marriage we had an encyclopedia of "looks." His "listen to yourself" was mildly admonishing and designed to force me away from rampant reaction and into thoughtful introspection. It worked.

Just one look and I knew I'd become bitchy and cranky because of my own feelings of inadequacy. It wasn't fair taking it out on Jon. So I shot him back my "oh crap, I see it now, sorry" look. And we were good.

Now I could concentrate on action steps that would answer the $64,000 question – had Ed been murdered? I thought that maybe if I made a short visit to see Detective Warren at the station house with my office cohorts, Peg and Babs, perhaps between us we could pick up on some irregularities or hints about Ed. That strategy would also help me accomplish my most important objective, to keep Eva and Abby from experiencing any more pain than they would anyway. I sent a quick email out to "my crew" and filled them in on Jules' suspicions and my carefully considered action plan. As I was finishing my email Jon came into the study to fill me in on plans for Ed's memorial.

"We got an email from Olivier," he started somberly, "the memorial service for Ed will be a wine tasting at Le Voltaire tomorrow night. We will feature wines nurtured by Ed and Abby, and each of eight of his professional chef friends will select and prepare a course that Ed himself loved to make, to accompany each wine."

"Really? I asked, "What a wonderful tribute to our friend." In that moment I had trouble understanding why funeral arrangements were anything other than a wonderful and happy tribute to someone we loved. A wine and food experience would be the perfect send off for Ed, nothing else would even make sense. I did feel a touch of guilt that the resulting feast would be phenomenal since Ed and Abby made awesome wine, and Ed had painstakingly collected the perfect accompanying recipes.

It felt somehow wrong to enjoy your friend's memorial service, but that feeling was indicative of our perceived need for suffering and guilt during times of mourning. Wouldn't it make more sense to seek solace and positivity in a time when mourning would reach out and grab you without your having to place yourself in inordinately unpleasant circumstances?

"That should be wonderful," I continued.

"I know," Jon agreed, "seems weird though, doesn't it?"

Jon and I agreed that it felt bizarre, but that was probably just because society had turned "the final good-bye" into something as painful as humanly possible, so it was the norm. We both agreed on the logic of changing that age old tradition; but breaking habits – even unpleasant ones – was not always so easy.

[CHAPTER 6]

The next morning was sunny and magnificent. Then, a thought of Ed made everything seem less perfect. With a heavy heart, I made my way to the kitchen to start the bull-dog breakfast parade. It was almost impossible not to feel hopeful while dodging a kitchen full of hungry and break-fasting bulldogs in an effort to sit down and eat your own meal. I was feeling better already.

I pulled into the parking lot across from the station house while keeping an eye out for "my crew." Naturally, Peg and Babs had beat me there. We assembled in the parking lot and had a 2-minute briefing before heading into the station to ask the desk sergeant for Warren.

"She should be back within 20 minutes to ½ hour," he informed us.

Damn! This was going to take longer than anticipated. I offered to treat for coffee at the Scooter's around the corner rather than hang around the station awaiting Warren's re-turn. The desk sergeant even agreed to send Warren around to join us if her schedule permitted. After we ordered and were sitting, sipping our hot cups of "waking up easy," Babs decided that she'd been hasty in passing up that offer of a scone; so she headed back to the line.

With one person ahead of her, Babs decided to peruse the glass counter filled with goodies. She moved from one side to the other, bending down to examine some of the more appealing treats. Apparently, Babs made her decision at just about the same time another customer entered the coffee shop. Unbeknownst to each other, Babs was crossing to regain her rightful place in line, while still leaning in to examine her chosen delicacy, at the same moment the afore-mentioned gentleman approached what he thought was the end of the line, Babs leaned down for a last look. The tall, raincoat clad customer smacked into her bent form with a force that lifted him up and over the coffee counter. He continued sliding across the counter slamming into both the barista and the large, scaldingly hot coffee dispenser, as Peg launched into action.

I sat stunned watching Peg propel herself onto the right side of the counter-surfing customer with significant force, resulting in sounds of bone crunching and glass smashing. Just as Babs lifted herself to a standing position, the surfer's feet swung around and hit her shoulder, propelling her toward Peg, perched atop the raincoated projectile.

I shrugged and rose, not sure of what, if anything, I could do to help.

By the time I reached the counter it was clear that the tall raincoat clad customer had been injured and was in a great deal of pain. Babs returned to a standing position, but as we worked to right Peg, she struggled to retain her grasp on her quarry. Before we had a chance to even begin to restore order, Warren arrived on the scene.

Oh shit! This was decidedly not the ideal way to accomplish our goal of discreetly digging for information about Ed's accident. Warren would be far less receptive as she witnessed another of our unfortunate and very public mishaps. When Peg, Babs and I travelled together there was usually carnage. This would be bad for all of us.

I pondered exactly what had happened here and what to do about fixing it, when something even more unexpected occurred. It started with a subtle change of expression on Warren's face. She went from annoyed and put upon to determined and aggressive as she sprang into action. In one smooth movement, Warren pulled out her gun and handcuffs. I was more baffled than ever. Was she going to arrest Babs and Peg?

As I stood by like a dummy, Warren took over possession of the counter surfer relieving Peg of her charge. Peg immediately turned to check on Babs and help her back up, while Warren pulled a gun from the surfer's raincoat and read him his rights. What the hell?

During the next several minutes I watched as Babs and Peg turned from klutzy and crazy co-workers to recognized public heroes. As it happens, Babs' earlier bumbling mishap had been more than a little fortuitous. Had the gentleman been an innocent customer, looking for his morning coffee, it would have been horribly embarrassing. In reality, when the eagle eyed Peg glanced over during the fray she caught site of a glimpse of a revolver and sprang into action. Once she spotted the gun, Peg dedicated herself to getting control of both the gun and the situation.

Thank heaven Warren arrived when she did, or I would inadvertently have thwarted Peg in her heroic efforts in order to minimize damage against the unsuspecting customer. As Warren explained before hauling her prisoner off to the station, when she first walked in she read the situation. On closer inspection, her carefully trained powers of observation turned to the raincoat, so out of place on a beautiful, warm, sunny day, and her suspicions were immediately aroused. It took another second or two before the glint of steel told her all she'd need to know. She had to stabilize the perpetrator and keep these courageous citizens safe.

Warren finished her arrest and her check for injuries that would require immediate treatment; no ambulance was called. We pieced together the last of the details for a full understanding of exactly what had occurred on that once peaceful morning. There had been a series of hold-ups over the past few weeks. A tall gunman in a nondescript raincoat held up convenience stores, fast food restaurants and coffee shops. His m.o. was to glide in quietly, pull his gun on the unsuspecting counter help and sneak out before customers even knew what had occurred. With no compelling or noticeable physical attributes, the raincoat was the only common and notable denominator – and Warren was no slouch.

Warren suggested we give her a ½ hour for processing and then head over to the station to give her our statements. She paid the barista to serve us all cups of tea – since coffee had ceased to be an option.

By the time we reached the station, there were reporters with camera crews and photographers to interview Peg and Babs. I looked at them and shook my head. One thing I knew, life would never be dull.

Babs tried her hardest to direct all the attention toward Peg.

"I just collided with the guy," she insisted to no avail, "Peg is the hero here!"

I was so proud of "my girls." How often did a pair of meno-pausal women rise to stardom as the superheroes in their hometown? There they stood, Peg, diminutive with short flat hair and Babs, taller with a fluff of curls framing her face. They were both clad in their work uniform of jeans and t-shirts as they told their stories to the reporters. As the owner of the ad agency where both women worked, the reporters wanted a short statement from me. I was cool. I told them what Peg and Babs had done that morning to make the city safer for everyone was par for the course for these two amazing women. They did not just become superheroes this morning. We were beaming as we reached the offices of Marcel and an impromptu ticker tape parade for our con-quering heroes!

Just after lunch my phone rang.

"Okay Donna," our friendly police investigator, Warren started, "you had come down to the station to see me, right? What can I do for you?"

"Well," I began.

"Let me see if I can guess," she went on, "might this have something to do with the recent, tragic traffic fatality of a friend of yours? Are you starting to itch for another investigation?"

She was smart. I found that somewhat annoying in such a young, attractive woman. She held a high powered job as chief homicide investigator in the city of Omaha, and she was thin and beautiful with long dark brown hair. She had it all, the career, the looks, the sense of style AND brains. Enough already!

Actually, I really like Warren. I admire and respect her; she treats me with equal respect. Yes, she is a very intelligent young woman.

"Look Detective," I jumped in, "I don't, for one minute, see this as a game of some sort. Ed and his wife Eva have been good friends of ours for quite a while now; it's just that a mutual friend has suggested the accident was not exactly accidental. Believe me, I've had quite enough murder for a long time; but it's hard to ignore your friends when they reach out."

Having two of my less enjoyable acquaintances brutally murdered within the past two years was really more than enough. It was still tough to accept, even after working with the police to bring the killers to justice. Having friends murdered is just not something you get used to.

"Relax Donna," Warren assured me, "I'm just busting your chops. Your friend has the kind of instincts we look for in a homicide cop."

"I'll be sure to tell him," I murmured, "so Detective, does this mean Ed was murdered?"

"Let's just say that we're not ruling murder out entirely at this point," Warren confirmed, "we're not taking anything at face value in this case. And I wouldn't mind talking to that friend of yours, the one with good instincts."

"But Detective," I pressed, "that means you really think its murder, doesn't it?"

It's never easy to get the inside scoop on what a homicide detective is really thinking. They are masters at keeping things close to the vest. I get that they have to keep things "under wraps" to some extent, but not knowing if Ed had lost his life accidentally or to a brutal murderer was making me incredibly nervous, and anxious for Eva and Abby.

"Let's just keep an open mind," Warren went on in her matter-of-fact, but damningly non-committal manner. What could I do? But I was no quitter!

"Please Detective Warren, Ed's family is important to me. If there is any more pain and horror headed their way, I'd like to try to help in any way I can."

"Just keep your eyes and ears open, Donna," Warren

suggested.

In my book, that was as good as asking me to help with her investigation. It was going to be difficult keeping things discreet until we knew exactly what we were dealing with; I had no doubt that Warren had what it took to keep things quiet until it was time to go public. I just hope I could be as adept; I'd hate to make things even slightly worse for Ed's family.

Just as I was ending my call with Warren my partner, Liv, walked over to my workspace.

"Ready for the latest?" she began, "got a call from Clovis."

Of course you did. Clovis Cordoba Seville, a former Marcel employee (and I use that term extremely loosely considering all the work she didn't do while she was on board) could sniff out trouble and attention getting opportunities with frightening alacrity. Perhaps it was because she hailed from a family of Romanian gypsies who claimed to corner the market on voyeuristic ability.

It never ceased to amaze me that tiny little Clovis, with her waifish figure clad in boring but stylish garments all cut a size or two larger than her frail little frame required, creating the image of a shrinking woman, could elicit enormous angst by the mere mention of her name. Her big fluff of severely damaged over color treated hair added a tragic element to the shrinking body/growing garments persona. Although she was fully convinced she was hot enough to hold a paralyzing attraction for virtually anyone who gazed upon her fashion model-like countenance, Clovis was more than a little bit creepy. And once you added her screechy/sing-songy voice to the mix, it was like the exorcism of a haunting ghost who was reluctant to pass over. I shuddered just thinking of her – for so many reasons.

I steeled myself for the onslaught I knew was unstoppable.

"Alright, what's her deal?" I asked.

"She wanted to let me know you were showboating again," Liv shared.

I thought I detected the slightest bit of amusement.

"Showboating? Let me guess, how dare I submit to an on-camera interview without somehow managing to involve "her nibs."

"Bingo," Liv confirmed my wild ass guess, "and let me add, that's the fastest you've ever hit on the psycho "topic du jour."

I wasn't sure if I should feel pride in my deductive reasoning or fear that I was starting to understand how that twisted mind thinks. Best not to tax my brain in this manner; a good soldier always presses on.

"What else?" I continued. I could feel the dread mounting within.

"Ha, you know her well, Donna," Liv confirmed, that as I'd come to expect with Clovis, there was always a price to pay.

"She wants you to fix your oversight," Liv stated almost too calmly.

I racked my brain for a possible clue to her expectations.

If nothing else, Clovis was helpful in keeping the mind sharp and clear – always useful in the journey through menopause. This time I was just not landing anywhere at all.

"My oversight," I mused aloud, "so I should call the reporters and ask for a follow-up interview in which I lament I should have mentioned that all I have, and all I've become, I owe to this amazing and annoying little person?"

"Not quite," Liv smirked, "you've got the ridiculous part down, but you should indeed contact the reporters and tell them that Clovis had assumed that coffee shop would be the next target hit by the armed robber. She'd been stopping in for her morning coffee on a daily basis knowing that his attempt was bound to take place fairly soon. It just so happens that Clovis' alarm clock failed to go off this morning, so she got a later start than usual. The outfit she selected smacked of a wardrobe malfunction – don't ask – so another delay as she carefully selected the day's attire. Then the traffic lights; of all mornings for every light en-route to be red – this was catastrophic! By the time Clovis reached the street to begin searching for a parking space you were conducting the last few seconds of your on-camera quote – the quote that should rightfully have been hers!"

"Well, when you put it that way, I can totally see why it was my fault!"

"Clovis and I were both sure that you'd see it her way once it was explained to you. After all, it was probably her Romanian Gypsy telepathy that sent you to the coffee shop when she herself was unable to get there in time."

"No other way TO see it," I confirmed, "how could I have been so blind?" I struggled to conceal a double eye roll and a full body shudder.

"Clovis is completely ready to forgive you for missing the obvious," Liv kept right on going, "she knows you don't have the superior intellect for truly high level reasoning, and she believes that your chronic self-centeredness will always cause you to grab the limelight when the opportunity arises. As long as you see to it that things are righted now she will happily forgive you."

"And if I don't?"

"Knowing your questionable character, Clovis never expected you to embrace "doing the right thing," Liv countered.

Just as she was getting to the punchline there was a commotion in the vicinity of the front door – Clovis!

"Ah, there she is now," Liv nodded knowingly, "she just assumed it would take a personal visit to get you on the straight and narrow." And without skipping a beat, "Now get her out of here before all hell breaks loose. If the staff thinks she's doing anything more than passing through, we'll have an uprising on our hands!" as she marched into the nearest conference room and firmly closed the door. Sure, easy for her to say!

Busted! Set up, even. I glanced through the glass of the French doors in the conference room where Liv took refuge in order to give her my best "arctic chill" look. She would not remain totally unscathed from her duplicitous act! Sadly, my facial retribution was lost on Liv who was struggling to remain composed. Good one, my friend. You got me this time! Ever the good loser I turned toward an approaching tsunami of screech.

[CHAPTER 7]

"Hello Clovis, how are you doing today?" I offered. What the hell, why not start with humor.

It took a lifetime – okay it confirmed that five minutes can feel like a lifetime – for Clovis to fill me in on the myriad of disparate and disjointed information representing what was on her mind. By the time she was finished with her first salvo, I was in a massive disinterest induced attention coma. That did not help.

"Donna!" Clovis barked and shrieked at the same time, "are you even listening to me!?"

That was a tough one. It occurred to me that answering the question was a lose/lose proposition. I decided deflection was the best means of attaining all of my short term goals here.

"Clovis" I powered back, "let's go to Aroma's and grab a cup of coffee if we're going to discuss this, and I sense that we are."

With one short and commanding sentence I had killed a whole flock of birds with a single stone. I would move Clovis out of earshot of the Marcel staff who were laboring to get several "hot" jobs out the door; I would short circuit her whole 'keen and scene' floorshow. (This was more like a fervent hope than a given – a Clovis extravaganza would still be pretty embarrassing at a public coffee house should my strategy fail.) I had provided myself a built-in escape – "finished my coffee, gotta go" drink and run! I was pretty proud of myself.

"Not so fast, Donna!" Clovis virtually shouted.

Damn, so close. Why do I always jump the gun and pat myself on the back too early?

"What about Babs and Peg? They are certainly implicated in this little "steal the glory from the true hero" scenario!" she continued in her ranting.

Ah hell, they really were heroes; time to take a bullet for the team!

"I put them up to it, Clovis," I threw myself further under the bus, "they were just following my instructions."

"Of course, I knew that as well, Donna." Clovis showed visible relief as she congratulated herself on homing in on the culprit right from the start, "I'm just glad you're able to honestly admit your weaknesses and failings. However else will I be able to help you improve yourself?"

Man, I knew it would be a large caliber bullet – but I wasn't expecting the hollow-point exploding effect. As we walked to Aroma's, Clovis continued to enlighten me on why I had orchestrated my latest grab at her glory. I know I was feeling enlightened.

"So, of course, you would choose those little church mice

to be your co-conspirators," she happily rambled, "you could never successfully share the limelight with me. I mean who would pay the slightest attention to you if I were on the scene."

At this point I considered making a run for it. Clovis was borderline giddy by the time we reached the front door of Aroma's. Once again she had brilliantly foiled my attempt at shamelessly grabbing her well-deserved glory; as a bonus she had unearthed more evidence that I could never hope to get any attention as long as someone with her unparalleled superiority was on the scene. Thank god I wasn't listening!

Once inside we ordered our latte grande mocha ventes. Naturally, I paid since I already owed Clovis so much. We grabbed a table in the far corner – normally we would grab the luxurious leather couch and chair grouping whenever it was available – but with Clovis' diminutive form she kept sliding between the cushions and painstakingly extricating herself over and over. I could tell it was starting to get to her and she seemed about to blow. Personally, I thought it was damn funny, and it was a welcome break in my concerns over Ed, but all good things must come to an end.

I was determined to have one quick coffee and bolt with as much of my sanity intact as humanly possible. At the rate I was going so far, that wouldn't be a whole hell of a lot anyway.

We spent some time reviewing the events of the morning. I was not about to apologize to Clovis – for anything. Luckily, her narcissistic nature didn't require a response from any individuals unable to meet her splendor – namely me. So I sat daydreaming, and caught a word or phrase here and there. When my cup was empty I jockeyed for an opportunity to make my escape.

"Wow, Clovis, this has been so enlightening," I started with my best impersonation of someone in awe. The great thing about this reaction was that the level of self-centeredness that enveloped Clovis made this the expected reaction for pretty much anything she said. It was an all-purpose, custom-tailored response.

"I'm sure," she acknowledged, "but we're only halfway through with our agenda."

Uh oh, where was she going with this? And I was so damn sure I could make my great escape. I was afraid to even ask at this point, so I just waited. Luckily, Clovis moved quickly into the other half of her diatribe.

"I heard about your friend, Ed," she transitioned, "I think we both know it was murder, and I am in an excellent position to be able to lead this investigation. I wanted to initiate a discussion to see if I am confident in your ability to assist me as I solve this case for the police."

That was kind of a shock. Wasn't it always jarring to realize that two separate sides of your world intersected without your even knowing about it? It was especially surreal when it was any part of your life – and Clovis. In her larger-than-life view of herself, it was difficult to envision how anyone else could fit into virtually any picture that she inhabited.

"You knew Ed?" I ventured.

"Certainly, he was a local businessman and something of a wine authority wasn't he?" she responded.

I still wasn't putting the pieces of this puzzle together. It was hard to imagine what she and Ed might have in common. My mind searched for a path of less pain; should I question Clovis, letting her think I cared or wait and see where she was going with this whole thing – aside from being the focal point of everyone's attention.

In some ways, having the attention focused on Clovis could prove to be a good strategy, enabling me to do some sleuthing without drawing any undue attention to myself. Unfortunately, dealing with Clovis was always so much work, and I would shoot myself if she managed to pull Eva and Abby into her own personal little me-focused drama. I had hoped to protect them from further pain – and being around Clovis was almost a written guarantee of added pain.

Clearly the place to start was to find out the connection between Ed and Clovis; that would help me determine whether or not she'd be of any use. It felt strange to even think that way, but allowing an amateur stranger, an out-sider, into the solving of a murder would make everything more difficult. This was not just a game. Written threats sent to me during the investigation of Claire's murder were still very much in my mind, and they would serve to keep me on my toes, with a low profile in any future investigations.

"Ed was consulting with me on some of the audiences

for the new wine he and his daughter were planning," Clovis en-lightened me, "he knew he'd lucked out in finding some-one as knowledgeable about wine making and promotion in the Omaha area."

That struck me as extremely odd. Ed was the wine expert having worked in the restaurant and wine industries for most of his adult career. He had been responsible for build-ing premiere wine lists as well as selling premium wines. His was a knowledge born of hard work and exposure over many years. Clovis, on the other hand, had barely graduated from drinking over-sweetened white Zinfandel – in fact she may not have graduated yet. Her casual comment had my brain twisted enough to keep me quiet and let her continue. We might get there eventually.

"From the first time we met in my elevated position at the side of the Chancellor's wife during her recent charity wine-tasting, Ed has relied on my opinion for new products and the best means of marketing them."

Now a picture was beginning to form in my mind. Although I would have to make a few phone calls to confirm, based on my prior knowledge of Clovis and all of her acquaintances I was pretty sure I knew how this thing had played out. Ed's winery had supplied the wine at the Chancellor's wife's charity wine-tasting. It seems as though I could recall him mentioning that it was slated to be a pretty big deal. The memory of that conversation with Ed distracted me momentarily – it would be tough to accept the fact that I would never have another conversation with Ed. There would be no more intense wine discussions, no more biting and obnoxious jabs, it just made me want to sob.

These were the moments that reminded you – so painfully – that you've indeed lost a friend. I knew there would be many more of these moments before I could ever begin to accept this loss – and that made me sad all over again for Eva and Abby.

Clovis cleared her throat, reminding me that I could pretty well predict the "details" of her acquaintance with Ed. She'd been only too happy to play gofer to the publicly lauded Chancellor's wife, a woman Clovis followed around like a puppy dog begging for a treat. After meeting Ed, Clovis would have imposed her opinion on everything under the sun relating to the entire event. Naturally, Ed would be at his most charming best in the preparation and implementation of this high profile event. It was quite a coup for Ed – a society wine tasting gig. The fact that Ed would be polite to anyone associated with the grand event would be totally lost on Clovis who only noticed how she was treated. As used as she was to being "brushed off," Ed's polite, if disinterested, attention would goad her into thinking he genuinely appreciated and sought her opinion. So she'd lose no chance to chime in and give him her views on literally everything!

I had to stop for a moment at this point. If Clovis really was dogging Ed and blathering endlessly at him – one had to consider whether or not his fatal accident might, in fact, have been suicide. Who knew he'd have such a strong motive.

"Fine, Clovis," I was finally ready to chime in myself, "so what do you think happened to Ed?"

"Oh, I know he was murdered," Clovis was quick to assure me, "and I know why."

"What do you know?" I demanded.

"Don't be so pushy, Donna," Clovis admonished me, "remember, I am taking the lead in this investigation!"

"Screw the investigation, Clovis," I barked, "spill your guts, or I will."

"Fine, Donna, but this is just one more example of how very difficult you can be, why I...."

"Clovis!"

"Fine, Ed and I met for lunch a few days before his tragic accident. We were at Le Voltaire and..."

"You and Ed made plans and had lunch together?" I demanded.

"Well, it might be more accurate to say that I had heard him mention, to the Chancellor's wife, that he had a luncheon at Le Voltaire on that day, and my friend Leesa and I just happened to be passing through..."

That made more sense. A world where Ed and Clovis were meeting for lunch just did not jive with me. This was so like Clovis, inserting herself into plans made by virtual strangers who would never consider including her. I was starting to wonder if this was not just a huge waste of my time.

"Well as I was saying," she continued unfazed, "Leesa and

I were sitting at the next table. Ed's phone rang and when he answered it his luncheon companion used the opportunity to visit the lavatory, so I may be the only person to have heard Ed's half of the phone conversation. Donna, it was clear that Ed was extremely agitated. There was a major disagreement and a bit of choked yelling; then it was clear that the person on the other end of the line had said something that really aggravated Ed. He went white as a sheet, and then kind of gray. When his lunch companion returned from the bathroom, the rest of their lunch was considerably subdued, although I could tell that Ed was struggling to keep his emotions under wraps. The other guy asked Ed a few times if he was alright; he finally admitted to feeling a little sick, said he thought he'd caught the flu from his next door neighbor – he'd brought the guy some chicken soup because he'd been too sick to get to the store himself."

"Clovis, can you remember any of the things that Ed said to this mysterious person?" I grilled her excitedly.

"Hmmph, not really, now that you ask," she responded distractedly.

"Well think, think hard!" I pressed, "this could be critically important!"

"Yes, Donna, I can see your point," Clovis became far more interested as she began to realize that remembering some of Ed's conversation could catapult her into the midst of all the attention.

"I just can't think now, Donna," she lectured me, "not

with you badgering me like this!"

"Clovis!"

"Look Donna, I understand the importance of remembering anything I can. It's not like I'm a novice at murder
investigation, I mean I did solve both Claire's murder and
B.J.'s murder, even though you have managed to grab all the
glory connected to both. Thank goodness for you I do NOT
have a large ego, always demanding all the attention!"

That's right, she solved the murders and was happy to let
me take all the credit; who wouldn't believe that?

"Alright here's what I'm going to do," she began in preparation of her big pronouncement, "I will go home tonight
and meditate in an effort to recreate those brief moments in
my memory. I will write down anything that I recall and
share it with you first thing in the morning. How's that?"

Although it would mean another encounter with the one
person I most liked to avoid – I didn't see an option. I agreed
to Clovis' offer, we said our long-awaited good-byes and went
our separate ways. I had a few more phone calls to make
before retiring for the evening I faced with mixed feelings. I
always looked forward to a wine tasting at Le Voltaire. I knew
with the combination of Ed's careful attention to quality
Hungarian style wine and food, and the fact that it was
prepared by some of the best chefs anywhere, chefs who
would give this particular feast extra care, we could expect
an unparalleled dining experience. My trepidation was the
doubts I had in my ability to maintain a stoic countenance

in the presence of Ed's family and close friends – menopausal emotional turmoil did not make times like these any easier.

[CHAPTER 8]

As we entered Le Voltaire I could feel the butterflies in my stomach promising to make this a challenging evening. It was to be expected under the circumstances. Olivier had shut the restaurant down for business – it would be a night dedicated to Ed and the things he loved most in life.

Looking around I could see the whole gang was here, but the joy and anticipation that could normally be read on their faces and in their demeanors was noticeably lacking. Even the two, or four, cheek kisses that had become our standard greeting was administered in a lackluster fashion. The overall gloom was exacerbated by the large number of strangers who were obviously Ed's business contacts and clients in the area. We'd only been there for about five minutes at this point, and I glanced at my watch in an attempt to track the painfully slow passage of time.

I would always look back on that evening with a measure of fascination. What started as a morose and weighty burden magically evolved into an evening that would hold cherished memories for many of us. The palpable emotions we'd all been struggling with since learning of Ed's tragic demise fell victim to an evening with close friends as we bonded even further over his life and the things in life he enjoyed – wonderful Hungarian food and wine that represented his origins as well as the Hungarian-esque vineyard he and his daughter had started together. Had anyone told me that, by the end of the evening, we'd be laughing and hugging and sharing stories of Ed – which typically contained some chuckling at the antics resulting from his bizarre and twisted sense of humor – I would have called them a liar. But I would have been wrong.

Initially, however, I labored to greet everyone as cheerfully as possible and to keep from breaking down this early on. Although it was not easy, I fared better than many on that front. The more friends I saw dissolving into tears, the more difficult it was for me to avoid joining them. It's not that I was ashamed to be crying in front of my friends at a time like this, it's just that I knew if I started now there was a good chance I'd ruin the evening – at least for myself. For me, crying elicits a chain of events – none of which enhance how I look or feel. First I fight them back as hard as I can, and then they begin to sneak out. Sneaking leads to pouring, and then it's difficult to find tissue that will keep the deluge from soaking my 'outfit du jour.' Once finished, I'm left with a big, red puffy face devoid of make-up (save for the odd streak of mascara drawing a nightmarish passage down my face) and a hopelessly clogged nose.

As I viewed my normally very attractive friends, it was clear that Ed's passing had taken a toll on all of them. It wasn't just the dour expressions that even the best of efforts could not alter to look positive, there was an unnatural pall over each of them that altered their whole look from facial expression to full body posture. I was walking among the undead, and I was one of them.

Fortunately, within ten minutes of arriving, three or four of the wait staff in black and white began passing among the guests and handing out Ed's recently released sparkling pezsgö wine. Like a growing number of quality producers in Hungary, Ed was opting for the champagneois method of producing his sparkling wine, rather than the traditional charmat and transasée methods. Ed had set aside a small patch to dedicate to his pezsgö, growing more obscure Juhfark, Királyeánkya and Kéknyelü grapes expressly for his pet project. The result was extraordinary. He always referred to the pezsgö as his private stock. Things were looking up. I had read that in the Hungarian culture the meal is often started with soup rather than appetizers and hors d'oeuvres. And tonight, it would take a little sparkling wine before we'd be ready to eat anything.

The next time I checked my watch forty-five minutes had passed. It's amazing how much more relaxed one becomes with a few sips of sparkling wine. I even managed to laugh at a joke that our friend Francois had shared; it wasn't that funny so I had to assume that nerves and bubbles were ruling the roost. My nervous giggle served to remind me of the import of the occasion but I felt no pangs of guilt for my expression of amusement; Ed would never approve of a sullen group of weepy mourners. On some level, we all knew that the only way to truly honor him would be to have a fabulous evening and laugh until the wee hours. In addition to mourning Ed, it was probably the fear that we wouldn't be able to muster enough positivity that had made us start out in such a morose manner – but if anyone knew how to liven up a party it was Ed – and his sparkling wine didn't hurt that effort a bit!

I was halfway through my second glass when Eva and Abby arrived. They each grabbed a glass and joined in the party. God, they had guts. Once Ed's family arrived it was time to start the toasts. As the night progressed the frequently raised glasses started out as beautiful tributes to a much loved relative and friend and digressed to an unintelligible babble. That is to say, as the wine flowed the inhibitions disappeared.

We sat down to our first course of Fisherman's soup or Halaszle. It was a hot, spicy paprika-based soup that went perfectly with the Tramini, Gewurztraminer clone, from Ed's vineyard. As I ate this light but commanding course I was reminded of Ed's love for all things paprika. I assumed that Eva had chosen the menu and Abby had selected the perfect wines to accompany each course. What a loving way to commemorate this man. I wasn't sure if I was more choked up by the sentiment or the spice.

As we made our way through the various courses and

accompanying wine, we shared memories and joy as well as a fair amount of tears. All in all, it was a wonderful commemoration of Ed and his life and a way to ensure that we all knew how very much we enjoyed and appreciated each other. It's unfortunate that it often takes tragedy to remind us of how very fortunate we are.

Our second course was a selection of stuffed peppers, some hot for the more adventurous in the crowd. As this course was served, Nic explained that they would not normally offer hot stuffed peppers after a spicy soup course, however, this particular dish was one of Ed's absolute favorites. Abby chose two wines for this course Hárslevelü and Kadarkz – depending on whether the diner selected the hot or mild peppers. Naturally, I felt compelled to try both – peppers and wines. What better way to honor Ed?

As I ate my way through the delectable peppers I gave myself a break from the conversation which gave me that rare opportunity of really being able to listen. In and among the reminiscences, I did overhear the odd comment about Ed and some kind of investigation. The abundance of wine did not aid in my ability to strain out the stroll down memory lane and concentrate on this new information. By the end of the course, I was convinced our friend Cal thought he had information that would lead to the killer. I half hoped he was wrong, for his own sake.

Our main course was authentic Hungarian goulash. A thick and hearty stew served with potatoes and a basket of rustic bread. The wine was a lovely Furmint, which is the most well-known and commonly grown grape in Hungary's legendary Tokaji wine region. While the rest of the world recognized that Tokaji produces one of the world's greatest dessert wines, Ed, typically never satisfied with the status quo, used the Fermint grape to produce an exquisite, fiery dry wine that elevated the goulash to a religious experience. I tucked into my goulash and ignored everyone around me. I guess I needed a bit of a break. When I came back up for air, I saw Eva making the rounds of mourners.

Eventually, I found myself talking to Eva. There are only so many times you can express your sorrow without sounding like an annoying broken record. We found ourselves discussing the plans for Ed since there were no plans for a formal funeral. Eva outlined Ed's carefully planned final wishes. His ashes would be transported to his vineyard and would be incorporated into the firepit so that he could return to the soil that he loved.

After a moment of silence, Eva made it a point to introduce me to Tim Iremont, the GM of Ed's Omaha distribution center. Although I'd never met him before, Tim appeared to have an odd look on his face. Maybe he was just sad, or did I detect a hint of guilt? Ah hell, maybe it was all the Hungarian wine. It was time to turn off the gumshoe and try to enjoy the good in this evening.

Dessert was a choice of Chimney cakes or Kurtoskalacs and an Esterhazy tort which consisted of five layers of almond merangue and butter cream with fancy swirls on top. They even offered a poppy seed bread pudding. I couldn't help but think that, although these desserts would all be delicious, they would have been better had Ed been here to make them himself. Abby's dessert wine, a very special Tokaji, made every dessert taste even better. Though very different, each dessert was an incredible confection rivaling the best Bavarian pastry.

The mood had changed dramatically. Certainly tongues had been loosened by the overabundant wine, but it was more than that. The specific selection of food and wine comforted all those who sought to spend just one more evening with Ed. We felt as though we had.

[CHAPTER 9]

The next morning, I didn't rush to get into the office. I lingered over a second cup of coffee and checked my emails from my small den off the kitchen. Surprisingly, the most interesting communication of all was a short email from Clovis.

"I remembered."

This may be a first, I was actually looking forward to talking to Clovis. I emailed back suggesting that we talk while I was still at home. Ever the showman, Clovis was not about to pass up a dramatic opportunity, so we arranged to meet downtown for lunch. That decision did give me more than a little unease. Maybe I could convince someone else to come along; but who did I like little enough to deliberately inflict Clovis upon them? I honestly couldn't think of anyone, so I'd have to go it alone. That called for a third cup of coffee.

I responded to the more urgent of the emails and returned all of the calls from that morning. When I hit the showers, I'd already achieved a sense of accomplishment; some days that never comes even when you're so busy it feels as though the day went by in a blink. It was another gorgeous day, so I borrowed Jon's convertible and treated myself to a leisurely drive downtown. The balmy air felt great; it smelled wonderful until I hit 80th street and was assailed by all of the fast food scents that greeted me on my journey down Dodge. By the time I hit 72nd Street I was craving a burger and fries. This would never do! It was still a long way until lunch where the best I could hope would be for a robust salad with a tangy fat free dressing. Ironically, even if I had indulged and treated myself to a big juicy burger and some crunchy golden fries – the resultant heartburn would render me useless and burping for the rest of the day!

Craig and Lake greeted me as I turned the corner and entered the wide open loft space where all of our workstations resided. They were working on a new website feature to manage the generation and chronology of leads for one of our major clients, and they had just set up a meeting to review some of their solutions before implementing them. I could sense the pride in of some of their particularly innovative enhancements, the ones that would ensure the client a custom-tailored deliverable that would work far more efficiently for them than anything already on the market. Since the meeting was set for 10 am, I had to hustle to get a few emails out the door beforehand.

I was back at my desk by 11:30 precisely. That would give me enough time to respond to two voicemail messages and the twelve emails that had accrued since 10 o'clock. By noon I realized that two of the emails would require some further work before I could prepare a satisfactory response. No time for that now, I had to get going if I was going to make my lunch with Clovis. I grabbed my pocketbook and dashed through the kitchen to the back door. Clovis had chosen Stokes for lunch. The downtown Stokes was just a few blocks from the Marcel office, so I chose to walk since it was such a lovely day.

I had to pick up the pace in order to get there by 12:10, so I was a little out of breath when I reached the front door. No problem though, I could easily see Clovis before reaching the hostess stand. She had chosen a table in their al fresco dining area so we'd get to enjoy the beautiful fresh air for a few hours. Aside from the fact that I would be dining with Clovis the prospect appealed to me enormously. Stokes had a nouveau Tex/Mex cuisine, and if things got too painful, they also had an excellent wine list.

As I sat opposite Clovis she greeted me with a sweet-ish hello and a smirk on her face. Apparently, I hadn't been forgiven for stealing her limelight. There was one very freeing thing about dining with Clovis; her bizarre moods did not conform to anything resembling logic – so there was really no way to figure out how to elicit the correct response. You could say the one thing you were sure she'd want to hear, and she would end up furious and launch a full out attack, or burst into tears. If you said the one thing you were sure would elicit an adverse reaction, she might run over and give you a great big hug. Knowledge of these landmines rendered trying to manipulate or control the dialogue pointless. So I didn't. I would just say whatever I wanted. How often in life does that happen?

When I first started out in the ad business, lunching at a trendy eatery like Stokes would automatically include a novelty drink or a glass of wine. Over the years, the trend toward healthy lifestyles has enveloped the ad industry – always first to fall victim to the "in" trends – and now alcohol at lunch is virtually unheard of. Listening to Clovis for the first three minutes of our lunch date prompted a rapid-fire response from me when our waiter asked "can I get you ladies anything to drink?"

"Do you have Sauvignon Blanc by the glass?" The words virtually leapt out of my mouth before I even realized what I was saying. I hadn't planned on imbibing over lunch. Oh well, what the hell, spending time with Clovis was always better when the edges could be softened a bit. Remarkably, when our waiter lamented that they didn't have a Sauvignon Blanc by the glass, Clovis came to the rescue.

"Let's just share a bottle, Donna, I'm sure we can finish it between the two of us."

Would you look at that Clovis, the perfect luncheon companion – except for some of those other things that made her impossible to tolerate.

Once our wine was poured we each ordered one of the signature salads. Mine was with avocado and shrimp and Clovis' was with chicken and black beans. I allowed myself to enjoy a few sips of wine before launching into a conversation that may or may not inform, but was sure to aggravate thoroughly.

"So Clovis," I began with no small amount of trepidation, "tell me what you remembered about the conversation that made Ed obviously upset at his Le Voltaire lunch."

"Well Donna," she responded with furrowed brows, obviously contemplating her assessment carefully, "at first I had no idea what was making Ed look so strained and unhappy. It was difficult to make out what he was saying because he'd moved away initially, and then after a few moments, he somewhat furtively moved even farther."

"So how were you able to hear anything then, Clovis?" I asked with growing concern. If she dragged me out for this lunch under false pretenses I would belt her one! Although I had to admit that, so far, the beautiful day and the lovely wine were not strong indications that I would end up being miserable before this lunch was over. Maybe only frustrated and annoyed – that was something to hope for.

"Well now Donna, don't you go being so impatient here," Clovis lightheartedly reprimanded me. Since when had she picked up a slight southern cadence? The woman took pride in her west coast/east coast seeming demeanor the majority of the time. Could this be an act? What was I thinking, could anything Clovis did be anything but an act? What difference did it make? I started thinking the wine was getting to my head a little too quickly. I looked around to see if our salads were on the way. Not yet. And then Clovis continued.

"You know me, Donna, always wanting to help my fellow

human beings any time I can spot someone in need."

Actually, that's not exactly how I'd put Clovis' interaction with other human beings, but we'd never get to her point if I interrupted for every little nuance in her story. So I held my tongue; perhaps it would be more accurate to say that the Sauvignon Blanc held my tongue for me.

"When I saw Ed looking all upset and nervous," she continued, "I figured I'd try to see what I could do to help the poor man."

"So you moved closer in order to eavesdrop?" I asked matter-of-factly.

"Now Donna," she snapped, "that man was clearly in need of some help, and who better to help than someone with my advanced intelligence and experience? I'm sure even you are able to see my logic here, Donna."

"I do," was all I had to say to get her ruffled feathers smoothed and her story moving forward. Sometimes I don't take my own best advice. At least she'd dropped the southern lilt.

"From what I could gather, he was speaking to an acquaintance and a fellow wine distributor about another wine distributor with whom they were both close. It appeared as though the fellow on the other side of the phone had suspected their mutual friend, a guy by the name of Ron, of selling some of his wine for cash and pocketing the profits. He had contacted Ed to share his suspicions and ask Ed to help him find the evidence to confirm that his suspicions were true."

"Interesting," I interjected, afraid to say more and push Clovis off course.

"I know," she beamed at me from across the table, "and it gets better. It became apparent during this conversation that Ed had done a bit of snooping; he felt Ron had played a little fast and loose in his current position. He'd been careful, but he'd undoubtedly engaged in some illegal behavior. According to Ed, during every fourth or fifth wine tasting, Ron would claim that a bottle was corked, and sometimes he would claim that a bottle had been broken, when neither had occurred. By implementing this method carefully but regularly, Ron had been pocketing a nice, tidy little sum. While Ed was concerned, he didn't feel that it was the federal case that his other friend was implying. But shortly before the end of the conversation, his friend clearly told Ed that he had found evidence that Ron had gotten lazy, had taken his little scam to an extreme, and would land himself in prison if he was discovered.

Ed was shocked. He tried to refute what his friend was saying, but he didn't seem to be gaining any ground. I can't be sure, but I get the general impression that with the evidence both Ed and his friend at the other end of the line had found, they were going to give some thought to confronting this guy and forcing him to stop."

"Wow, Clovis, that's really something," I acknowledged with respect, "that certainly indicates Ed was involved in some tense stuff within the last few weeks of his life. I have to give you credit for your sleuthing skills."

"Well Donna," she went on as if I thought I could ever stop her, "I'm glad to hear that you acknowledge which one of us has the intelligence and street smarts to gather important information on a murder investigation. I mean the thought of you fancying yourself even an amateur sleuth, when someone with my capabilities is so close to the action, well dear, I'm sure you're not unused to being laughed at on a fairly frequent basis."

I was fairly certain that was not what I had said.

I thought for a moment. We were on the sidewalk just a few feet from a very busy road. Was there any chance I could propel her in front of a fast moving vehicle without being detected? It didn't look good – but it might well be worth the risk!

Sadly, there's not much point in trying to debate Clovis on issues of this sort. She was clearly the superior being to everyone around her – especially me, as she pointed out as often as humanly possible. The really amazing thing here was that I honestly didn't believe Clovis knew she was being insulting. Why would anyone be insulted at being reminded that she was superior to them; after all it was just a matter of fact!

At times like these I would often resort to my overflowing bag of lethal barbs, or a verbally delivered practical joke. I never said I was above retribution, and since logic was pointless it was my only chance at getting a shot in. This time, however, I opted to let the whole thing pass over me like water off a duck's back. Any other rejoinder on my behalf would only serve to lengthen the time I would be stuck with Clovis. No, better to let this one pass and extricate myself as soon as possible given the limits of physics.

"Anything else, Clovis?" I asked in an attempt to wrap things up and move on.

"Not really," she responded, "he seemed in command by the end of the call, like I remember him from the Chancellor's wife's wine tasting. Did I mention that she was adamant I be there as her honored guest, Donna? After I helped her with all of the planning, she said she really couldn't enjoy the actual event unless I was also there enjoying myself. I could hardly say no now, could I?"

From my vantage point, I had garnered every piece of valuable information I would get from this lunch, eaten my salad, drunk my two glasses of wine; now to get the waiter's attention and get that check ASAP. I'd have a chance of escaping with minimal abrasions and contusions to my psyche.

"Can I get you ladies any dessert?" our overly chipper waiter asked.

"No thanks, we're full, and we'll need the check ASAP," I delivered in a rapid fire drill designed to get him to see the urgency in my need to leave. Thank god it worked!

We split the check, said our good-byes and I was back in the office in time for our 1:30 new business meeting. No time to really contemplate the information that the brilliant and talented Clovis had imparted; maybe tonight over some wine on the deck!

[CHAPTER 10]

The afternoon went by in a blur. I finished searching for some secondary research on animal behavior, and it occurred to me that I was thoroughly enjoying our decision to get more involved with marketing to support animals and animal related products. Afterward I signed expense reports and checked emails before writing a post for our marketing blog. I always preferred writing posts on ad campaigns that missed the mark in one way or another; lucky for me there was no shortage of those, and they were my best shot at writing humor during the work day. On rare occasions I was also able to blog about campaigns that I really enjoyed and they were typically humorous themselves. While I may not have been the one writing the humor in those instances, I would always enjoy giving credit for a talented use of humor where credit was due.

By the time I reached home that evening I was ready for a nap. A hectic day and a bottle of wine for lunch had taken its toll; not to mention the added stress of dealing with 'the queen of me!'

As I walked through the door I was greeted by the welcoming bulldog parade for attention, along with a heads up from Jon; we were having some friends over for some wine and a light supper on the deck. I shot him a quick look to see if he was kidding – he wasn't.

"Oh god, Jon, I hope I don't fall asleep with my head in my dinner plate!" I was starting to panic.

"Relax Donna," Jon assured me, "I told them to be here at 7 in case you wanted to try for a brief cat nap before their arrival."

"Oh thank god," I sighed while diving for the couch in the family room. Jon knew me too well. A short nap and I should be good to go for the night! In the meantime, I knew that Jon would take care of any of the necessary prep for our guests' meal. If I took a short nap I could join in the preparation – of the house, the deck and the meal – and if my body decided I needed a longer nap, our guests would have to settle for my dazzling personality and a delicious meal cooked by Jon. Either way I didn't think they'd mind.

I awoke after about fifteen minutes full of questions about our guests and our meal. It seems that Jon had run into Phillippe La Plage earlier that day and they got to talking about what had really happened with Ed. Phillippe mentioned he'd also been talking to Cal Fiesty at the memorial and they both agreed that the details of Ed's demise seemed "off" and required some deeper investigation. Jon figured it wouldn't hurt to get the group together for a social evening, and if something helpful came out of it in terms of getting some closure on what really happened to Ed, then – and he hesitated before declaring that it would "kill two birds with one stone." I winced, he blushed.

Knowing the theme of the evening, I decided I'd better make my rounds both inside and out to at least ensure the most pleasant possible surroundings for a dinner that could head down one of several unpleasant trails. I felt certain that just being out on our back deck on such a magnificent evening would be enough to keep the spirits up during some fairly heavy dinner conversation.

Our deck was in such a beautiful setting. Perched above the hot tub room, it was a story above the ground floor surrounded by a variety of trees from evergreen to Ginkgo Biloba. The deck itself featured a built-in bench along one of the short sides and up part of the next with built in planter boxes. The boxes were filled to overflowing with a variety of greens and flowering plants. A guest at one of our first deck soirees best described the experience when he said "it's like being in a tree house." He was right, I always felt as though I was peering through the boards of a tree house as I looked down on the neighboring yards.

We completed the outdoor lounging and dining experience with a lovely wooden table that fit snuggly up to the built in bench – complimented by modern aluminum chairs on the remaining sides. A pair of aluminum lounge chairs near the grilling area completed the furniture arrangement. The gas grill itself was nestled into the far corner to keep the heat of cooking as far from diners and loungers as possible; a downright brilliant design choice for some of those really warm Nebraska nights.

I could smell the beginnings of Jon's preparations. He had selected a simple but elegant antipasto and would grill tilapia and sea bass for the main course, along with a medley of vegetables and fresh seafood risotto. Having a gourmet cook for a husband has its benefits – which can also be its drawbacks for the perpetually dieting, menopausal woman! But then, I suppose, healthy overeating is better for you than loading up on yummy tasting garbage! At least that's what I always tell myself. I had finished primping around the house and deck. Just as I was thinking I wish I had some kind of floral piece for the table, Jon's telepathic skills jumped into action.

"I grabbed some flowers when I ran to the store earlier, they're in little plastic vials so I left them in their wrapping paper. Take a look and see if you can use them in your décor for the evening."

He never ceased to amaze me. Once located, the floral wrapping revealed a lovely spring mix of daffodils, tulips and irises. They were perfectly suited for the makings of a spectacular centerpiece. I could already envision the fragrant blooms centered on a table filled with delectable foods and wine amidst a backdrop of cascading flower boxes which were backed by a virtual forest. I couldn't think of a more idyllic setting. Okay, make that with the possible exception of cocktail hour on a pool adorned deck perched high above the ocean, overlooking waves crashing down over an outcropping of rocks; but remember, this is Nebraska, no waves.

Our guests, Phillippe LaPlage, a charming gentleman born and bred in France and brought to the U.S. by the hospitality business, escorted his lovely wife Jeannie, a clever MidWestern entrepreneur and horse rancher, and Cal Feisty, a retired surgeon with his R.N. wife Jane, a pair whose unbridled humor was reminiscent of the legendary Burns and Allen comedy team, arrived precisely on time. A fact which never ceased to surprise me, having been born and bred in the northeast, where arriving on time was considered a declaration of one's lack of savvy. Personally, I felt that timeliness was a tribute to one's host and I really appreciated being able to count on my guests' punctual arrival. Many a meal has been compromised by the haphazard arrival of the east coast chic!

And true to form, both the La Plage's and the Fiesty's showed up bearing wine and delicacies to share. Their incredible graciousness never faltered, but it too was an entrenched part of the way of life in the heartland. We greeted like long lost friends even though we'd dined together the prior evening. The loss of a good friend tends to tighten the already close bond of friendship. Plates and wine bottles were dispatched so we could head out to the deck for our first toast of the night. It was another fitting tribute to a lost comrade. Phillippe's solemn homage to Ed was followed by an involuntary moment of silence, which was broken when

Jane shouted "Come on, don't let the shrimp get cold, it's a new recipe I had at a party last month. Let me know how you like it."

That was all we needed to dive into our hors d'oeuvres and wine with enthusiasm. We sampled and sipped for a few moments as we caught up on our lives. No mention of Ed or Eva was made aside from the toast, for the first half hour or so. This is such a typical characteristic of human nature. Establish normal before immersion into the painful or difficult. It was almost as though we'd been taught that, if you can establish a base of normalcy, you can handle the difficult things that come your way. I didn't know if that were true, but I had seen this behavior play itself out so many times before that I felt there must be something to it.

Feeling happy and relaxed we settled down to begin some serious conversation. Phillippe was well aware of his son, Jules, phone call to me regarding his suspicions that Ed had been murdered; so we started our conversation with Phillippe, filling Jane and Cal in on Jules' concerns. Cal was quick to jump in and assure Phillippe that he had reached that conclusion on his own. It seemed as though everyone was eventually coming to the same conclusion. There had been no accident.

As I listened to my friends detail the clues that lead them to these conclusions, I couldn't help but wonder if any other group of friends of a guy like Ed would do the same. I had my doubts. It was difficult for me to ascertain whether the available facts would naturally lead any group of intelligent individuals to such a conclusion, or was it possible that these, my friends, tended to have murder on the brain? Don't get me wrong, I don't fancy myself as their thought leader; it's just that the folks who know me have been around murder and murder investigations far more than the average individual. I wondered, was it rubbing off on them? Would they see murder everywhere they looked from now on?

I could just envision the conversation in our future social gatherings.

"Phillippe, I heard that your great aunt Gisele just passed away in the nursing home at the age of a hundred and eight. Do they think there was foul play?"

Or

"Jane, that patient you were nursing, the one who had his second massive coronary, just died, didn't he? Do they suspect the wife?"

Had I inadvertently created a monster, or was there just an inordinate amount of murder surrounding me? Hmmm, come to think of it I wasn't really sure which scenario I preferred. Jane asked me a question dragging me back from my reverie.

"I said, have you talked to the authorities yet, Donna? What do you know?"

"I have and not much."

I proceeded to fill them in on everything I knew. What little there was only served to convince them they were on the right track. I couldn't fault them because I had to agree. As the evening progressed, I realized Cal had some additional information that would prove to be very enlightening. Apparently he had been in an investment group that had backed a number of wineries, all from Napa. Cal's group used one distributor and offered cross promotional opportunities. It was kind of a new business model and they weren't sure if it would prove successful yet.

Cal mentioned that at their last investor's meeting there was a puzzling disparity in the distributor's balance sheet. It had been identified by one of the CPA's in the group a few months earlier, and the distributor had glossed over it with disdain. Unfortunately for him, this particular CPA was not so much mousy but more overtly aggressive – he wasn't letting go easily. When the investor group got wind of the problem they were of one mind; don't overly alarm the distributor yet – but get to the bottom of the problem. Their way of doing that? Enlis t Ed to investigate.

Ed was a guy they all knew and trusted. He was well known throughout the wine industry. Having Ed kick your tires was nothing new to vintners and distributors alike. The problem was, he was getting ready to make an interim report on his findings – if there were any – when his accident occurred. Cal said, so far, no evidence of anything he might have found, one way or another, has been unearthed. That did not bode well.

Cal was quick to qualify that there were still some stones

that had been left unturned; by that he meant, evidence might well exist in the home Ed had shared with Eva for over thirty years but not one of those brave investors was inclined to disrupt a widow in her time of grief to look for something they couldn't even identify. That would come in time. The problem was, if such evidence did exist, it would be critical to any murder investigation that might be underway. This was going to be tougher than we thought. Not one of us could imagine the thought of venturing into this unthinkable area with Eva if it were not absolutely necessary.

As the evening went on, Jeannie had a thought that the rest of the group adopted.

"Donna," Jeannie started, "since you've been speaking with that Detective Warren, why don't you call her tomorrow and share Cal's information? Odds are it's not something she's heard yet since the investor group is pretty close."

"Oh yeah, Jeannie, that makes perfect sense," chimed in Jane, "because she might be able to do some checking on her own without upsetting Eva, and with her professional training she'll be better equipped to inform Eva of their suspicions when the time is right."

With the resounding approval of everyone around the deck table it was settled. I would be contacting Warren again in the morning.

For the rest of the evening we relaxed, visited, laughed a little and did our best to shake off the sadness that still engulfed us. We had a last glass of wine and packed up, making it an early evening for everyone. Some of us had early mornings to look forward to, and all of us were more than a little drained from Ed's memorial the evening before. In retrospect, I felt this dinner party had probably saved us from a fairly morose evening had we been left to our own devices. I was grateful for the company of our friends. And I was glad not to be alone in what promised to be the most difficult murder investigation of my short, but active, sleuthing career.

[CHAPTER 11]

First thing the next morning I had Warren on the phone. I outlined Cal's intelligence from the previous evening; I also gave her the rundown on Clovis' eavesdropping. True to form, Warren was most appreciative of the "inside information." She said they'd been formulating a strategy for infiltrating the investor group in the event that something had been amiss – but they hadn't gotten very far to date. She also thanked me for filling her in on Clovis' "take" on Ed's phone call; without my even asking she assured me she would never "rat me out" to Clovis. If for one moment, Clovis believed I stole her thunder by passing on a piece of vital information, my life wouldn't be worth a plug nickel! Then, uncharacteristically, Warren cracked a joke; and I cracked up.

"Actually, now that I think of it, Clovis probably did tell me already..." Warren started out in a way that had me a bit perplexed, "it was probably in one of the one hundred and forty-two emails she has sent me in the past three days. I kid you not, one hundred and forty-two. So I think you're good!" she finished, with what I could only imagine was a shit-eating grin. Great! Smart, beautiful, thin AND funny – the rest of us just didn't stand a chance!

It was a good way to start the morning; I felt like an exemplary community citizen for helping save the investigators valuable time in a murder investigation. I also felt good about doing something for Ed, even though he'd never know it. Now I was sad again. And I was pretty sure it wasn't just a dip in my menopausal hormones.

Before I had a chance to sink deeper into my solemn reverie, I realized Peg was standing by my side.

"Donna, it occurs to me we should probably take a look at Ed's car before the evidence is destroyed. Look, I know this will be especially hard for you..."

"You're absolutely right, Peg," I interrupted with renewed energy, "do we know where it is?"

"Yeah, I tracked it down to a scrap metal yard just a few miles outside of the city," she responded without skipping a beat, "and I understand they plan on crushing it before the end of the week."

"Then we'd better plan a road trip at lunch today," I declared, "it would be foolish of us to ignore what could be an important piece of the puzzle."

My conversation with Peg had renewed my sense of purpose and re-energized me. I flew through my morning tasks with a speed and precision that surprised even me. If every day were like this, I could work full time, run for office, learn a foreign language and write a book! What were the odds?

As I was finishing up my last task before gathering the

troops and heading over to the junk yard, my phone rang. It was Eva. After an initial greeting and another outpouring of caring and concern, Eva got right down to business.

"Hey Donna," Eva began, "it's come to my attention that you have been asking a few discreet questions in relation to Ed's accident."

Damn! I didn't want it to happen like this!

"Not really, Eva," I hastened to assure her, "some things have come up in passing."

"It's okay, Donna," Eva reassured me, "I can't tell you how much I appreciate your intentions; your loyalty and friendship mean the world to me. I just don't want to see you waste any of your valuable time. You have so much on your plate already, and I want to reassure you I know for a fact that Ed was not murdered."

"Oh, of course, Eva," I responded with as much perkiness as I could muster (and that was a tall order for me, even on a good day), "I can't tell you how relieved I am to hear that. It must be comforting for you to feel so sure."

"I am that sure, Donna," she assured me.

"I have no doubt that you are, Eva, "I acquiesced.

After hanging up I was back to feeling sad again. I suspected that speculation on the possibility of Ed being murdered would be difficult on Eva; I had no idea she would go into a total state of denial and refuse to even consider the possibility. Eva was a smart and resilient lady. If that's what she needed in order to get herself through this tragedy and move on with her life, I would do everything I could to support that and protect her from dangerous wagging tongues – including mine! I had to admit to feeling a little bit surprised. Eva was such a pragmatic person; it was hard to reconcile her refusal to consider the possibility. But grief was a very strange thing and you couldn't predict how you would react when the time came.

By the time Eva and I hung up it was time to rally the troops for our road trip. As I turned my head I could see that Peg and Babs were standing at the ready so I grabbed my bag and we headed out to the car. Peg took a few moments to give us a rundown of the types of things we could hope to find in our search. She acknowledged it was possible the most we'd get was a better understanding of what may have occurred logistically. Odds were any trace evidence would have been gathered by the police in their initial investigation of the crash.

We made it to the junk yard in fifteen minutes flat. At this rate we'd be able to enjoy a leisurely lunch before heading back to the office. Why was it that my head always went to the nearest eating opportunity? Ah hell, some things would never change.

I could see by the look on Peg's face she had noticed that traipsing through this maze of sharp metal garbage could potentially be hazardous to our health. She glanced at my shoes, black fashion shoe-boots with a three-inch heel; oh well, at least the heel was wide. She rolled her eyes; apparently the wide heels did nothing to appease her concerns for my safety. After glancing at her footwear, as well as the soft suede boots on Babs, Peg realized I was not the only problem. None of us were in any shape to be tackling the land mines ahead of us, but she knew that wouldn't deter us for a second.

We all stepped forward tentatively and picked our way through the debris. It was quite an intimidating pile of rubble. I couldn't begin to fathom how we would locate Ed's mangled wreck. Just as I was starting to regret my hasty decision to check this place out – I had stumbled twice and nicked the tip of my black toe, damn! – Peg chimed in with the solution.

"We have to look for the little hut where the operator sits. He'll be able to direct us to Ed's car; let's hope it's not too much farther."

No sooner had she finished her sentence than the top of a small wooden façade came into view. It was just around the next mountain of scrap metal. Shouldn't take too long.

"Shit," I said as I twisted my ankle and landed on my butt on a pile of questionable rubbish. Thankfully, there didn't appear to be anything piercing my butt so I would probably only need medical care for my ankle.

As soon as I hit the ground, a pudgy little gentleman came waddling over to try and help me stand again. I took a quick look at his extended hands before grasping them to right myself. They looked clean. The balancing act that enabled this passable double for Wonderland's Tweedle Dee to restore me to my feet had certainly defied physics – and probably at least three more natural laws.

Once standing it was clear I'd strained or sprained some-thing in my leg. Just great, now I'd be hobbling over debris in ludicrous footwear with a bit of a hop and a limp. This was going well.

Peg and Babs scrambled over to do the requisite assess-ment of a fallen comrade. They fussed and fretted and brushed me off. In the midst of all of the unwanted attention, we managed to introduce ourselves to Mr. Pudgy, his real name was Fred Jenson, and explain our reason for visiting his "little piece of heaven."

With Fred's help, we made it to the location of Ed's car without further bodily harm. There was one problem though, his car was perched atop a mountain of metal at a height of about thirty feet. Peg, Babs and I just stood there with our mouths hanging open. I was about to suggest that we'd wasted valuable time, once again, when I spotted Peg from the corner of my eye. She was sizing up the mountain and appeared to be gearing up to have a climb. Luckily, Fred spotted her as well.

"Hold your horses there ma'am," Fred cautioned Peg, "ain't no need to go climbin' no junk mountain and get killed now is there?" When put like that, Peg could hardly argue the point. A climb up that mountain of metal scraps was not likely to end well, not for a twenty-year old smart ass, and certainly not for a menopausal office manager.

"Well Fred," Peg started her debate..." But Fred was way

ahead of her.

"We have ways to get folks up to the top without riskin' their lives, ma'am. I mean we take safety very seriously here at the scrap metal yard," Fred proposed with surprising eloquence.

"Well how …." Peg wasn't ready to give up yet, but Fred was just too quick for her.

"We got ourselves a bucket loader. We use it when the higher layers of metal need to be examined. You know those layers of metal, with nothing to hold them in place, are just an accident waiting to happen if you get to climbin' on 'em. Believe me, we learned our lesson the hard way."

"Well break out the bucket loader," Peg smiled with anticipation, "I'm ready to go for a ride!"

It took Fred a few minutes to prep the bucket loader for a jaunt across the yard, so Peg, Babs and I were left standing by ourselves contemplating our next move. I looked up at the mass of metal that had supposedly been Ed's car and started to feel a little queasy. I think it was the combination of seeing "the" car, my recent injury and the fact that I might be suspended in a plastic bucket over a field of crushed and twisted metal at any minute, that brought on my increasing malaise.

Babs looked over at me.

"You don't have to go up in the bucket you know, Donna," as she, once again, successfully read the situation. "Ya look kinda' green from here."

"Oh hell no," Peg concurred, "especially not if you're feelin' as bad as you look. Of course, I'm guessing your curiosity will overcome your seasickness by the time ole Fred gets here with that loader. After all, you are the one who's likely to be most familiar with Ed's car; and I know you'd hate to get all the way over here and miss the opportunity to locate any important clues. Clues that will be lost forever if you miss this chance."

She had me there. There was no way I would miss this chance and live to kick myself forever. Time to suck it up and pull myself together. By that time, Fred was making his way over to us and I could see that this "plastic bucket" was actually pretty substantial. Maybe it wouldn't be so bad after all. And let's face it, there was no way I was going to take the chance this car would get crushed and take with it the answer to our mystery.

It was determined that Peg and I would go up in the bucket. Once up there, they would have to lower the bucket if we felt we needed to view the wreck from another angle, it made more sense than trying to move the loader itself. Fred was not about to risk a safety violation by moving that loader with the bucket high up in the air. Actually, I found his little safety lecture to be quite comforting. He really did seem to know what he was doing.

I took my own sweet time climbing in. Fred assured us that mine were the first pair of high heels ever worn in this particular bucket; who'd have guessed? Once firmly entrenched, Peg and I gave the high sign and the bucket slowly started its ascent. At first it was pretty cool. It felt almost as though we were viewing a new art installation at a museum. All that twisted and gnarled metal in all those different colors. After what seemed like an eternity we made it to the top of the twisted mountain, and there was Ed's car, looking decidedly worse than the last time I'd seen it.

So many thoughts flew through my mind. I was having trouble accepting that this could even be Ed's car. It's so funny how the human mind works. When tragedy strikes one is forced to accept it on so many different levels – and one can never be sure of the reaction along each step of the way.

Peg looked at me with concern.

"Donna, maybe this wasn't such a good idea." She was looking extremely skeptical. "I think that, once again I have bulldozed you into something you just weren't ready to handle; I'm so sorry."

"No Peg, I will do this. It just took my breath away for a second there. Now let's start to look for anything at all that might be helpful, even if it seems meaningless right now."

As Peg and I were doing our best to examine Ed's mangled car, Babs was just as busy checking for clues from where she stood below.

"Hey guys," she yelled up, "isn't Bohóc the name of Ed's winery?"

"Yeah," I confirmed, "that's right, why?"

"Well, there's a box down here at the bottom and it has

that name on it," she calmly informed us.

Peg and I just looked at each other and shook our heads.

"Babs," Peg calmly ventured, "is there anything IN the box?"

"Looks like some papers with a bunch of chicken scratch on them. Like a stash of secret papers, I'd guess," Babs concluded her speculation.

"Well hell," I declared, "we might as well come down if that's where all the action is! Please lower us, Fred!"

Babs, who had been stooping, picked the box up and began to stand upright. Unfortunately, she chose the very moment that Fred was making his delicate move to lower the bucket. As Babs stood, her back bumped up against Fred's elbow, the one on the controls. There was a momentary jerk and the bucket started to flip. Peg and I looked at each other in horror and grabbed on for dear life. Once the bucket was fully upside down, Peg and I searched frantically for a stable looking section of scrap metal on which to stand – clearly neither one of us had been masters of grade school gymnastics!

In the scheme of things, I think I was luckier than Peg. She did a bit of a somersault and trampoline routine as she made her way all the way down to the bottom of the manmade mountain. Thank the lord she never made contact with hard metal. I am guessing that she stopped at the drugstore for some lice shampoo on her way home, since her head must have hit a dozen different and moldy car seats in her descent.

I, on the other hand, managed to find a perch that held me in place until Fred was able to right the bucket and save me from a possible fate worse than death. Not taking any unnecessary chances I eschewed gracefulness and dove head first into the bucket and safety. Upon arriving on the ground, they fished me back out and I managed to bang my injured ankle yet again; thus ensuring that I would return home with a legitimate injury.

Once safely on the ground and calm, Peg, Babs and I thanked Fred profusely, grabbed our little Bohóc box with the secret papers and fled the dangers of the scrap metal yard.

We stopped at Methodist Emergency on the way home for an x-ray and an ace bandage. It was official, I had a sprained ankle.

[CHAPTER 12]

Once properly wrapped and medicated for the pain, I grabbed my new crutches and dutifully settled into the wheelchair for my ride to the hospital exit and freedom; well, sort of freedom. Jon had pulled the car up to the emergency room doors, Babs and Peg stood by to help whisk me away to get pampered mercilessly. At least that was the plan.

It was a short-lived fantasy. Babs and Peg assured me they, and the Bohóc box of goodies, would be following in Peg's vehicle so we could all examine the contents of our new found treasure. I had to admit, although the prospect of some intense pampering was tempting, curiosity over our find was just that much more enticing. What did that say about me? I shudder to think.

Our caravan turned the corner on its way home, when we spotted Warren's unmarked car parked out front. As we pulled into the driveway, Warren stepped out of the river birch shadow and opened the passenger side door in an effort to help get my drugged and gimpy self into the house.

"Heard you'd been injured in the line of duty, Donna, and I figured I'd come over to check on you myself," Warren offered. "Besides, I wanted to pick up the Bohóc box before any of the contents had a chance to go missing."

Damn, I didn't see that coming! Why didn't I insist on rooting through the contents during all of that time between x-ray and wrapping? Major rookie mistake! As these thoughts flitted through my mind, I realized that Babs and Peg were nowhere in sight. Had they spotted Warren's car and realized they'd have to relinquish our find? I noticed Warren picking up her head in a casual check of the area. She didn't seem concerned, and then I noticed why. Heading toward us was yet another caravan; this one consisting of Peg's vehicle, followed by a cruiser with lights flashing. Busted!

Warren smiled as Officers O'Dowd and Riley pulled up to the curb behind an innocent looking Babs and Peg. Within seconds the officers took possession of the coveted box and headed off toward the station. A dejected Babs and Peg made their way over to us.

"Nice try," was all Warren had to say.

"Yeah, ...huh?"

"What..."

Neither Babs nor Peg had a convincing excuse nor did they have the energy to invent one. Sometimes it's just best to admit when you've been busted and move on with your life.

"But can we at least..." Peg began.

"No promises, but I'll share anything I can once we've reviewed the contents." Warren was starting to get good at this mind reading thing.

Once settled inside with my ankle propped up and an

ice pack on the lump, I was starting to get drowsy. That was probably just as well. I let Peg spar with Warren over our recent misadventure and the potential consequences. I knew I'd be hearing the Jon version in a more lucid moment and no one likes repetitive lectures on the dangers brought about by stupidity, especially when it's yours.

I must have dozed off because my next conscious moment occurred long after the crowd had cleared out and Jon, Jasmine, Roxi, Sadie and I were alone. I stayed conscious long enough to eat a nice bowl of Jon's chicken soup. It was so comforting. No wine though; Jon wasn't taking any chances with the heavy-duty pain pills I'd ingested earlier. He was unwavering in his vigilance. This was going to be a long recuperative period.

After a deep drug induced sleep, I awoke refreshed but hurting. I struggled to get up and balance on my new crutches; it wasn't pretty. After quite a bit of stumbling and fumbling, and no small amount of cussing, Jon convinced me to abandon all thoughts of heading into the office. We agreed that working from home and getting used to my new balance made sense for the day. I have to admit, the thought of working in my jammies did have a certain appeal.

Once the bulldogs showed their unanimous approval of the day's plan, it was a done deal. I hurried to my computer so I could let the crew at the office in on my whereabouts. Replies to my email indicated that the office concurred with the bulldogs and felt that home was where I needed to be.

Sheesh, everyone's got an opinion!

Easing into the day, I wrote a lengthy blog post on 'sprained ankles and the menopausal woman.' You definitely sweat more when you're hopping around and trying to navigate with crutches. The real challenge is that pretty much everything, during menopause, is a guarantee to sweat more.

Once my post was uploaded, along with a photo of me and my infirmity – ala Jon – I moved on to check for new emails and voicemails and found there was nothing urgent.

I hobbled upstairs to take my morning shower after carefully encasing my sprained ankle in plastic. If felt good to be clean again; I powered up and dressed in my most comfortable sweats.

Back at my desk, I decided that this would be a good day to begin compiling the list of what I knew about Ed's untimely demise. There appeared to be a lot of loose ends, but nary a thread to tie anything together. Naturally, due to Ed's career and lifestyle preference, the major common denominator was wine; that seemed like the best place to focus my list.

I made columns indicating what aspect of wine in Ed's life fit with each of the various clues. It seemed like the best way to organize the facts since, if any two columns turned out to have a major tie it would be easy enough to lump them together on the spreadsheet. I had a column for past employers in the wine industry, one for contacts related to the winery, Bohóc, another for clients and vendors of Ed's Omaha distributorship, one for acquaintances and competitors and finally, one for family and friends. It was interesting to see an active and well-balanced life that was so thoroughly immersed in all things wine. I felt fortunate that, in addition to our interest in wine, Jon and I also had a major focus in bulldogs and skiing. I couldn't imagine facing a hung over day when the only thing around me was wine and more wine. I guess you needed to really learn how to control your consumption when wine was such an all-consuming part of your life – at least you'd better! Although, truth be told, it always surprised me how infrequently anyone in our large circle of wine-loving friends ever showed any signs of over imbibing. Somehow, we seamlessly managed to pace ourselves and stay in control throughout even the longest of evenings; that did not, however, deter us from arranging for a designated driver on most of the bigger party nights.

I remembered my early days in advertising in the northeast; I saw more displays of embarrassing drunkenness to last me a lifetime. It's not like I'd never seen it before, my parents were big partiers when I was a kid. It's just that these folks clearly had little regard for their careers and their futures as they stumbled their way down the hallway, blatantly hitting on any warm body in their path (and we're talking both men and women – alcohol did not discriminate as it selected it's 'fool du jour') and stopping occasionally to relieve themselves of their stomach contents. It was not my fondest memory.

After years of witnessing alcohol as the master, it was encouraging to be part of a group that deliberately held tight control of the reigns whenever alcohol was invited to the party.

As I was finishing my murder/wine clue list the phone rang. It was Peg and Babs checking on my welfare. They're so considerate! Oh and they were wondering if I'd heard anything about the contents of that box. It helped bring me down to earth a bit learning that the two most considerate women in the world were still more concerned about satisfying their curiosity than they were about my welfare. Hmmmpphhh!

After assuring my peeps that I had no more knowledge of the box contents than they had I was able to get off the phone. I responded to a few emails and made a few phone calls before Jon beckoned me for a homemade bowl of 'comfort soup.' So far, my experience of working at home was feeling like a smart thing to do, not just because of my infirmity but in general. I was so comfortable and without constant interruptions it felt as though I was getting a lot more done. Better not get used to this, a lot of folks can function in a vacuum, but in an organization that relies heavily on collaboration, working in isolation was destined to defeat the whole purpose. Once in a while it didn't hurt though.

I spent the rest of the afternoon writing and researching. By about 4:30 I had gotten an enormous amount of work done. Now would be a good time to give Warren a buzz and try to weasel some information out of her on the contents of the infamous box. Normally I was pretty good at weaseling information, but Warren was a formidable adversary in the ever frustrating quest for clues.

I called and waited a good ten minutes before they were able to get her to the phone. She must have been in a good mood because she was immediately forthcoming with some valuable intel, either that or she figured it was the best way to shut me up and I would never know what else I didn't know. Needless to say, I would continue to wonder what the good detective was holding back.

"Donna, how's the flipper?" she started in good spirits, "don't tell me, let me guess, you want to know what treasure was in Ed's box of secrets."

"Well, I'd be lying..."

"Yeah, I know. And I don't blame you," she continued still in good spirits, "after the trouble you went to to find the information, the least I can do is share information about the contents with you."

"Really?" I asked.

"Sure, I don't think it will hurt anything," she replied, "the box was filled with notes Ed had made on any number of things connected to his business, including those guys he was unofficially investigating for his colleagues."

Now my curiosity was at a peak; that little tidbit had made me hungry for more. I wondered how hungry I'd remain after hanging up.

"So," I began tentatively.

"So we haven't read through absolutely everything yet, but we've seen evidence that he had uncovered some major issues on both investigators. In fact, if we looked no further there would be plenty of motive for several of these guys to kill him; the question is: did they know what he'd uncovered? That will be a major focus of our investigation moving forward."

"No kidding? We really found a box with a boatload of motive all tied up in a nice little bow?"

"Yeah, as a matter of fact that's exactly what you stumbled upon when you and your girls went crushed car surfing. In all seriousness, I want to thank you for rescuing what could well be the most important evidence of this case a mere hours before it was slated for incineration. You may have unwittingly saved our whole case."

Unwittingly? Did she really just say we did that unwittingly? I would beg to differ, Madam Detective, I fumed. Normally, Detective Warren and I pretty much saw things eye to eye. I can't remember ever getting angry at her through two prior murder investigations in which we collaborated. But to say that we risked our lives in the hope of finding the very evidence that we did find, unwittingly, was going too far. It was totally wittingly!!!

"Now don't get me wrong," she continued before I had worked myself up into a full head of steam, "I don't mean to suggest you found that box by accident. I just mean you were checking out a longshot and happened on major pay-dirt. The team and I are grateful that you took the initiative and it paid off so handsomely."

Well now, that was better. Amazing how you could go from wanting to pop someone to wanting to hug them, and all in the space of a few seconds. It was a valuable lesson for me. Don't shoot your mouth off before you've heard every-thing there is to hear, which is my typical m.o. Just think how foolish I'd be feeling if I'd ripped into Warren for that use of the term 'unwittingly' before allowing her to finish her thought and turn the whole thing around. Hmmm, I was going to have to give some thought to self-control in the future; that would really cramp my style.

I was very proud of myself for showing some self-restraint. We said our mutually appreciative good-byes and got off the phone before I realized I hadn't really learned any of the details of the motives that were strong enough to firmly place several suspects on the list. Damn! So busy congratu-lating myself I didn't ask the next most obvious question. That was when I had to ask myself, was Warren's use of the word unwittingly and her subsequent backtracking to avoid offending me just a ruse to distract me from pressing for further details? Damn she was good! Well played my public official friend, well played!

[CHAPTER 13]

Over my glass of Kim Crawford Sauvignon Blanc that evening I was feeling somewhat despondent. The ups and downs of this case, the thrill of making an important contribution and helping to move this murder investigation forward, combined with the suspicion that maybe I wasn't as great as I gave myself credit for, were really exhausting. Exhilarated one minute and embarrassed the next – that really ate into the confidence I needed to keep going on this thing. Just as I was rethinking my conversation with Warren in a borderline desperate effort to find the rationale that would exhilarate and help keep me pumped for the duration, the phone rang. Jon answered the phone and brought it to me with a puzzled look on his face.

"Hello?" I asked tentatively.

"Donna Leigh?" began a raspy but somewhat familiar voice.

"Yes, this is Donna Leigh."

"I've got some information that will help crack this case wide open," he rasped, "you need to come out and meet me in the parking lot by Millard Junior High," he continued, "back where the trees are thickest; be there at 10 sharp and come alone."

"BULLSHIT!" I responded.

"Excuse me," he rasped with a hint of surprise before continuing in a more menacing tone, "I don't think you understand me, lady! I have important information that will never see the light if you don't…"

"BULLSHIT," I interrupted.

"Wait, lady," he tried to recoup.

"Let me explain something to you, Raspy," I began with vigor, "what kind of moron do you take me for? I am NOT taking orders from some unknown nut job trying to entice me into a ridiculously dangerous and completely vulnerable encounter."

"But lady,"

"Don't 'but lady' me," I continued warming to my righteous indignation, "what do you think this is, some dime store murder mystery? I don't give a fat rat's ass what information you have! As much as I want to help solve my friend's murder – I can't bring him back by placing my own life in danger, so just get that out of your head! If you've got nothing better GET OFF THE PHONE AND STOP WASTING MY DAMN TIME!" I bellowed, perhaps a tad too vehemently.

"Okay, so now what?" he asked.

Would the killer ask me that, I wondered?

"Now why don't you drop the chicken shit voice disguise; man up and identify yourself! Then maybe we can discuss next steps."

"Alright, alright," he pleaded in his normal voice. It was Tim Iremont, the general manager of Ed's distribution business in Omaha.

"Jesus Tim, what were you thinking?" I asked completely exacerbated, "were you trying to scare the ever loving crap out of me?"

"No Donna, I'm real sorry," Tim offered sheepishly, "ya know I knew you'd never be in danger by meeting me," he assured me.

"That may be, Tim," I acknowledged, "but I had no way of knowing that, now did I? So wouldn't I have to be pretty damn stupid to agree to something without knowing if the jackass that wanted to meet was just an idiot or a full blown axe murderer?"

"Well, when you put it that way, Donna, I can kinda see why you're so angry now," he admitted.

"Alright let's move on," I announced, "what do you have for me, Tim?"

"I know that you and your crew found that box when you went to see Ed's car," he started in a maddeningly slow build. This was going to take a while so I shifted my weight, put my sprained foot up and got comfortable. "But what you don't know, Donna, in fact what no one knows, is that Ed kept the really damning evidence in a locked drawer hidden away in the largest wine storage section of the distribution warehouse."

Now it was starting to get interesting.

"Yeah," he went on more confidently, "the stuff in that box was related, but not the key to what he was investigating. He always worried that his car could be broken into and the important stuff would disappear, so he took steps to make sure that wouldn't cost him all of his hard work."

"Interesting Tim," I gave him some props for getting to the point, finally, "so what made you call me?"

"I didn't know what else to do, Donna," he admitted, "I didn't want to upset Eva, and I knew if I went to the police they'd only contact her anyway. I figured that you would want to protect Eva too, and I knew that you had a working relationship with homicide in this town; it just seemed like the right thing to do. Can you help me?"

"Sure, Tim," I agreed. I could only hope the curiosity did not really kill the cat. "But first, we'll need to review the information to ensure that it's worth the attention of homicide," I stated with certainty.

"Oh sure, that's probably a good idea," he acknowledged, "when do you want to do that?"

"How about tomorrow at noon? I can meet you over there before my lunch at Le Voltaire," I offered. Jon did not know it yet, but I planned on working from home again the next day – and getting him to drive me to Ed's warehouse and then out to lunch at my favorite Omaha restaurant.

"Yeah, that works, Donna. I'll meet you there at noon tomorrow," Tim finished with obvious relief.

Once our plans were made I settled back to finish my

wine, eat my standard meal, consisting of a fresh vegetable and a diet frozen dinner, and fill Jon in on the plans to convince him I deserved a nice lunch out for everything I'd been through. Luckily, it wasn't too tough.

When we arrived at the warehouse the next day, Tim was leaning against his truck waiting. The first few moments were slightly awkward, undoubtedly due to his embarrassing performance when he called the night before. I worked to put him at ease, after all, he was trying to do the right thing even though his first attempt was just plain stupid.

Tim let the three of us into the wine storage area and took us to the very back of the largest room. He moved a few stones out of the old and crumbling wall and low and behold, there was a locked drawer. Tim had availed himself of the key already, so it was only a moment before he opened the drawer so that we could get on with our investigation.

"Well, huh?" Tim uttered as he peered into the drawer, "that can't be."

"What is it?" Jon and I both exclaimed.

"The lock is broken and the drawer is empty. That can't be," Tim mumbled to himself, "it can't be."

"It's empty?" I asked.

"It can't be," Tim repeated,

"It is," Jon confirmed as he peered in himself, "completely empty."

"Ed must have emptied it before the accident," I offered.

"He didn't, he wouldn't break the lock." Tim responded.

"But it's empty," I reminded him, "Maybe the lock jammed and he was in a hurry."

"Donna, I spoke to Ed on the day of the accident and he had no intention of emptying that drawer."

"He could have changed his mind," I offered.

"You didn't hear him, Donna," he wouldn't have changed his mind, I just know it."

"Well Tim, if that's true, it means that somebody else broke the lock and emptied the box," I helpfully pointed out the obvious.

"That's just it, Donna; Ed and I were the only two people who knew about the drawer. And I sure didn't empty it."

"Stolen?" I mused.

"Not likely," Tim responded, "how would anyone have known to look here? Ed was always very careful not to let anyone see him access the drawer, and it was so well hidden; I think there's very little chance that it was stolen."

We were getting nowhere fast. Now we had a mystery within a mystery. Puzzling, but there wasn't much we could do at this point, and my ankle was beginning to throb. I suggested we all head over to Le Voltaire for a nice relaxing lunch. We agreed not to mention "the drawer" to anyone we happened to run into at the restaurant. No point in dragging other people into something we didn't understand ourselves.

We arrived at Le Voltaire for the last blush of lunch. As soon as we were seated, Nic walked toward us with his typical welcoming demeanor. Nic Hayes was the head waiter at

Le Voltaire. I smiled in anticipation of his charming and witty greeting and was surprised to see his expression change from joyous greeting to something that seemed furtive and watch him veer off course and toward the bar. What the hell was that? It appeared as though he was thrilled to see us until he noticed Tim at our table. Was I right about that? Was it Tim that caused his sudden shift, or one of us?

"Did you guys see how strangely Nic is acting?" I asked hesitantly.

"How can you tell?" responded Tim and both he and Jon chuckled.

"Neither of you just saw that?" I asked more determinedly.

Apparently they hadn't; was that just male obliviousness or had I imagined Nic's strange behavior?

Nic's metrosexual persona gave him the ideal credentials. He was clearly knowledgeable about fine food and wine, he absolutely oozed snarky charm that was both cool and trendy. Nic could charm the birds out of the trees – both male and female. He was a walking goldmine for a restaurateur.

Nic could make you feel urbane, chic and delightful; with a sharp snap of his sensibilities, he could make you feel like the biggest goofiest dork on the planet. He had power over others; thankfully he used his power wisely, most of the time.

I turned around and looked at Nic behind the bar. When he noticed my stare he looked up, waved tentatively and quickly put his head down to focus on his task, definitely not typical behavior for the man of charm. Jon and Tim chatted away completely unaware of my dubious thoughts. Life must be nice when you're tuned out to the weird vibes of the world around you.

Nic never did end up waiting on us that day. Tessa, the wait staff manager, and another good friend, ended up waiting on us herself. There was nothing unusual about that, Tessa was a "roll your sleeves up" kind of girl, nevertheless, I couldn't help wondering what provoked that behavior in Nic. I tried to be cool, find out if something had happened.

"So Tessa," I began, "what happened to our boy, Nic? I was sure he was on his way over to wait on us; it seemed as though he changed course mid-stream."

"Yeah? I don't know," Tessa returned, "he seems fine to me."

Well, so much for sleuthing here. This group was as tight as they come; they were trained to show a professional demeanor and ensure the customer a fabulous experience. It was so ingrained that they never broke rank, even when they were among friends. Not wanting to arouse suspicion I let it drop. I didn't think that Tessa had noticed anything; and I knew for sure that Jon and Tim hadn't. At this point I was starting to think that perhaps I had misread things. It's not always easy to know when to trust your initial instincts. I tuned in to the conversation at our table in time to hear Jon giving Tim some sound advice.

"So you think the empty drawer is worth sharing with the police?" Tim was asking.

"I do," Jon concurred, "the empty drawer could be an indicator of the murderer showing signs of panic; a panicky murderer is the most dangerous kind. You could be in some degree of danger yourself, Tim," Jon finished.

"Gee Jon," I admonished, "scare the poor guy why don't you!"

"It's okay, Donna," Tim assured me, "I can't pretend it's not something I've already thought of myself, in fact, I'm thinking it's time to beef up security both at my home and the warehouse. I'm starting to feel a bit vulnerable all of a sudden."

"What will you do?" I asked.

"I'm not really sure," he admitted, "I'll have to give it some thought and decide how far I need to go with this whole thing. I don't want to be stupid but I sure don't want to live in fear. Who knows if this murderer will ever be caught; I don't want to spend the next twenty years trembling in fear and hiding from the shadows."

We managed to have a pleasant afternoon. The food and wine were superb and we were finally able to change the subject to that of the most surprising wines over the past six months. Tim and Jon were totally engrossed in their topic. They didn't even notice when Suzette and Annabelle, the mothers of the Forstesque's, owners of Le Voltaire, came strolling through the front door for a glass of wine and a light nibble. I waved to the newcomers and motioned for them to join us at our table. By the time they got close enough to exchange pleasantries both Tim and Jon broke out of the intensity of their wine chat in order to grab a chair each and seamlessly seat our guests. Suzette was a chic and stylishly attractive European grand dam. Her Hermès scarves and fashionable, chunky gold jewelry were the perfect complement for her très expensive parfum. Suzette's elegance was discernible from the moment she entered the room. Annabelle, on the other hand, was a quirky and entertaining spitfire. Her wardrobe was just as fun and quirky as her bubbly cockney personality. She was a trendsetter in her own right. Her spikey strawberry blonde locks framed her petit and delicately featured face. Although very different in style, both women had an intense interest in the lives and welfare of their friends and acquaintances.

As soon as we were settled in and Tessa had brought additional wine glasses, both Suzette and Annabelle lost no time in debriefing Tim on life and business after Ed. It was fascinating to watch them pamper and fuss over Tim's loss; their ministrations brought Tim out in a way that neither Jon nor I had been able to accomplish in the few hours we'd been together. He positively beamed as he poured out his heart to these lovely and charming ladies. Jon and I both sat back and watched in admiration. I had to admit to feeling a bit inadequate in the presence of these notable masters.

By the time our guests had finished their appetizers and salads, Tim appeared to be feeling better about almost everything. I had to pay close attention to how they did that; I was certain it was a skill that would come in handy down the road. It was interesting to note that both women worked to maintain a support profile and enable their ward to take center stage; if they only knew how very much they just gravitated toward center stage naturally and delightfully. Life could be funny like that.

By late afternoon, we had finished our meals and began to express our good-byes. We wished each other well and each of us commented on our concerns for Tim, both physically and emotionally, each admonishing him to take extra care of himself; then we all headed our separate ways, none realizing how quickly our admonishments would prove prophetic.

[CHAPTER 14]

The alarm woke me from a dead sleep. I headed down to the kitchen in order to feed the bulldogs, and then myself. I'd just about sat down to my breakfast of designer coffee and sugar-free instant oatmeal when the phone rang. It was Warren.

"Donna," she started, "can I ask you to swing by the station on your way to the office?"

"Sure, am I correct in assuming that an important piece of evidence in Ed's case has come to light?" I pushed.

"I think that's a fairly safe assumption," she responded, "but it's not one we're happy about."

"I can't imagine that any important evidence would make you unhappy." Warren was sounding bizarre this morning.

"Got a call from one of Tim Iremont's neighbors at 2 am last night, music was blaring out of the open garage door" she droned mechanically, and my innate sense of alarm started tripping all the switches; I could feel a sense of panic start to rise up. "When we arrived on the scene we found Mr. Iremont's body. He'd been dead for about four hours."

I wasn't sure if I was sitting or standing. I knew I was beginning to hyperventilate. I looked at the phone, not sure of whether to listen, hang up or just drop it on the floor. That was when Jon walked in. He took one look at my face and obvious bewilderment and took the receiver from my hand. He led me over to the kitchen counter and onto a chair before talking into the phone. It didn't take Warren long to fill him in on the latest news.

From what I could ascertain, Jon had agreed that both of us would stop down at the station once we'd had a chance to treat ourselves for shock, shower and dress. It occurred to me that it could be quite a while before we made it to the station. I don't think I was cognizant of the fact that I was in shock, but I was aware that it was not normal to be seeing everything in slow motion and to hear things as though they were at the end of a long metallic pipe. I was pretty sure I wouldn't even risk showering until things returned, at least slightly, to normal.

By the time we made it to the police station, we'd already had calls from several of our friends, all wanting to know if what they'd heard on the news was true. Unfortunately, due to shock and police discretion, we were not really able to give them anything other than to confirm that Tim had indeed joined Ed in the great beyond. With promises to all that we would brief them when and if we knew anything, we bolted out of the house immediately after dressing to avoid the rest of the calls that would inevitably be coming our way. One thing was certain, our communication chain was functioning brilliantly; our callers, to a man, were aware of our marathon Le Voltaire luncheon with Tim the day before. As we drove toward downtown and the station, it occurred to me that if businesses and government could be a quarter as accurate in their communicating, the world would be a far better place! Unfortunately, I did not see that as a strong possibility.

As soon as we walked into the station we were ushered into Warren's office where she sat with a sympathetic look on her face. As usual, Warren wanted every specific detail we could remember, and she was somewhat less than forthcoming in sharing the details of Tim's death. Not surprising in the scheme of things; I knew Warren would share as much as she could, but on some level, not knowing the details could serve me well down the road if either I should become a suspect, or if key information leaked out and I needed to be ruled out as the loose lips that slipped.

After our meeting with Warren, neither Jon nor I were in any shape to conduct our normal "affairs of the day." In fact, we weren't in much shape for anything other than staring into space. We stopped at the nearest coffee shop to contemplate and steel our nerves. There was little conversation.

Oddly, my head went to Donny Miller, a former Marcel partner. Donny had left about six-months prior under circumstances I would have to describe as unusual. After five years of working side-by-side and being business partners for four of those years, Donny announced one day he had to leave.

When Liv and I had brought him into the business, we

113

never imagined he'd be around for more than 3 or 4 years based on his career pattern. We had him pegged as a jumper almost immediately. At that time his name had been floated to us from a common acquaintance. Donny had an interest in starting a business consultancy division – not dissimilar from many of the things we already do – however, many prospects feel the need for a consultancy that is separate and distinct from their advertising and communication firm. With Donny we could give them that.

Unfortunately, we learned within the first six months to a year that Donny was a brilliant idea guy – but he was not an implementer. Try as I might to take the implementation off of his hands, he was too much of a control freak to allow it. Thus, there was no consultancy division. In many ways Donny was a welcome addition to our ownership group – he was a smart guy and he accomplished some difficult tasks. But then the difficult tasks became fewer and farther between, and Donny started to lose interest. That was when he started to wreak havoc on our staff and our culture. Donny required continuous affirmation that he was the smartest person, ever. Clients hated that as did staff. His methods of proving his superiority always came at the expense of others, and generally left him looking like an ass. Ironically, it was through these blustery displays that we began to learn he wasn't nearly as smart as we'd originally believed – and he certainly didn't play well with others. The more of us who saw that the Emperor had no clothes – the more agitated and dissatisfied he became. Consequently, things began to decline. Although his departure came as no real surprise and was, in fact, rather a relief, his reasoning was a bit thin.

On this day my thoughts ran to Donny because in prior murder investigations, his relentlessly competitive nature prompted him to create a contest to see who could solve the murder first. Although, in these contests, Donny never faired as well as he would later claim – he did get us all motivated to think the problem through; and among us we arrived at the answer before significant further damage could be done. In at least one case that translated to 'saving my ass.' For which I was eternally grateful. In addition, Donny was well connected in the city and could often get us information that was mission critical. Now, however, his two main sources of information, his high school buddies turned cops, Riley and O'Dowd – or Frick and Frack as we referred to them – were now contemporaries of us all since we'd plodded through two high profile murder investigations together.

I wondered what Donny was up to these days. Part of me wanted to call him, but he seemed to withdraw from any further contact with Liv and me. Perhaps shame, perhaps guilt, or perhaps a feeling of relief that he had escaped. We would probably never know. It occurred to me it had been a while – out of sight, out of mind, I guess.

At around this time I realized that Jon was speaking to me and starting to realize I was oblivious to that fact.

"Did you hear me?"

"Huh?"

"I'll start again."

"Do you feel up to going into the office now, or would you rather we head home?" Jon asked.

"I'll go in. Maybe it will distract me."

"Do you want to talk about what happened first?"

"We probably should. It seems as though the killer is getting dangerously close to us, and that does frighten me," I admitted.

"You'd be foolish not to be frightened," Jon replied. "I think we should have some ground rules for moving forward."

"Things like: don't be alone, especially at night?"

"Right, and don't even use the Ladies' room in a deserted, dark hallway in a public venue, at least not alone."

"That may be a bit extreme. I'll be sure to bring a long-pronged fork with me if I find myself in that situation. But I do appreciate where you're coming from with this – and I suggest that you conduct yourself with as much diligence."

"Agreed."

[CHAPTER 15]

My arrival at the office caused a huge disruption. Client and internal meetings alike were interrupted to grill me on my recent lunch with a more recent murder victim. It was somewhat overwhelming, but in a way it helped me to settle in and focus on the tasks at hand. Strange how those things can work sometimes.

At 11:45 Maxie strode by and announced that she, Liv, our CFO Cora and I were going to lunch together. We picked a comfortable haunt and ordered pretty much all of the comfort food on the menu. Murder was an excellent excuse for taking a break from the diet!

Partway through our spinach and artichoke dip, Liv declared, "We're forming a think tank. We're done with those stupid competitions of Donny's. They were unproductive and, frankly, divisive."

Now THAT was an interesting take on another of Donny's brilliant devices. Oh how the self-appointed great have fallen!

When Donny had been with Marcel, his hyper-competitive ego had driven us to compete for virtually every goal we needed to meet. Murder was no different for Donny, when each of the two prior murders had occurred, Donny had formed crime-solving teams within the agency in order to create another potential platform in which he could emerge victorious. These teams significantly cut into the productivity of our collective thought process and slowed everything down to a crawl. Now, Liv was suggesting that we handle our investigation with a far more collaborative approach. Brilliant!

So that's what we did. The four of us formed a murder think tank with the understanding that we would pull in key personnel as the situation warranted. We would work togeth-er, share information, and attempt to solve this murder, stat! Leaving egos at the door – okay, we'd at least try.

During our main course, we reviewed all the information to date and made some determinations. We agreed that Liv and Maxie would work on Cal's vineyard investment group and their concern over the books, and Cora and I would handle Ron, the fast and loose wine distributor involved in lord knows what nefarious business. It wasn't a contest; more like divide and conquer. We would share all of our findings and each group help the other with speculating, postulating and just plain thinking through the facts.

It was times like these that made me feel good to be alive – sorry Ed. I felt extremely fortunate to be part of such an impressive group of problem solvers – and genuinely good people. And we looked good to boot! Liv was in her character-istic fashion-forward attire. Today's outfit was a masterpiece in blocks and blue (i.e. there were varying shades of blue, and all in the shape of varying sized blocks). The background was a pale, pale gray matching her baby soft suede grey boots. And where the hell did she find earrings in multiple sized blocks in multiple shades of blue. Incredible.

Maxie, on the other hand, was chic in her black skinny pants tucked into knee-high black buckled boots and topped by a black and brown fringed poncho. Her blunt cut hair with poker straight bangs paid off the outfit in its fashionable, yet futuristic vibe. And last but not least, Cora sported a three-quarter length skirt in black with a chunky tan cardigan and coordinating black & tan scarf wrapped glamorously about her neck. Her sensible shoes belied some challenging hip problems.

Cora had the smooth, mocha complexion of a twenty-year old woman, when in fact she was in the same menopausal age range as I. Her curly mop of hair ranging from shades of subdued red to dark brown complimented her perfect and wrinkle-free face – damn her!

I, of course, wore all black. Black slacks with a black tee and a black jacket. Oh and don't forget the black boots – made of the softest leather with a flat heel – I wasn't ready for high heels just yet. Lucky for me, flats were in and I had enough comfortable ones to see me through my unfortunate junk-yard injury.

We each sported our own unique signature look, but when thrown together on a problem, we functioned like a well-oiled machine – with the occasional hiccup – okay, make that nuclear explosion. Hey, we're still human. I loved working with these women.

* * *

After lunch Cora and I agreed to spend about 20 minutes creating a game plan for our investigation. We started with a list. Cora felt that our first step would be for me to contact Detective Warren. She felt that a more intensive set of questions, directed at the contents of the box we'd found at the car impound lot, would help to determine whether or not anything in the box would prove to be relevant in our analysis of Ron's illicit actions, to which we now referred fondly as The Ron Chronicles. As she pointed out, if there's nothing in there for us we can let Liv and Maxie know so they can plot their box strategy, but if those papers connect back to Ron, that will be a major area of focus for us, at least initially. That made perfect sense, so I prepared to make the call.

Warren was out, so I figured I'd swing by the station at the end of the day to see if a face-to-face would net better results. Besides, my foot was finally starting to feel better.

The rest of the afternoon flew by and I was ready to head to the station to try and catch up with Warren. Peg saw me heading out and confronted me.

"I know you're up to something. Perhaps you'd better tell me where you're going," she insisted.

"Nowhere dangerous. I'm on my way to the station to talk to Warren."

"So naïve. A trip to the station may not equate to physical danger, but you know damn well you can get yourself into plenty of trouble. Babs and I are going with you! If nothing else, we can run interference."

I thought about some of their methods of running interference in the past – and shuddered. Arguing would be pointless. So I didn't.

We took separate cars and headed over. It took us several minutes to find decent parking, and then we all trudged in together – the three amigos! The desk sergeant took one look and rolled his eyes. Perhaps arriving as a trio was not the smartest move. Without our asking, he ushered us into Warren's office where the detective sat busily typing on her keyboard.

She looked up as we walked through the door. I thought I saw a mixture of fear and amusement on her face; is that even possible?

"Glad you're here, I could use a break from these mind-numbing reports. What's up?"

I would normally never go to the police station unless I had something to report, but after working two murders together, I figured our relationship could tolerate some variation. Besides, my greatest fear in the two prior murders was that I could easily be considered a key suspect based on my relationship with each of the victims. This time was different. I knew no one would ever believe I would kill Ed. As annoying as he could be, that was just not enough motive for murder. Besides, he was usually smart enough to stay away from my really hot buttons. As I said, he was annoying, not stupid. And I had only just met Tim when he met his untimely demise. With full confidence, I jumped right in.

"I know you can't reveal any details of the investigation," I began.

"Right."

"But I was wondering if you could help me understand something. That box of papers that we found at the car impound..."

"You're right, I can't tell you about the specific contents of the box, but as I've already told you: the contents included information about two different cases that Ed appeared to be investigating on his own."

My heart fluttered a little – SCORE – maybe?

"But those papers allude to the papers in the safe. The ones that were stolen. Apparently the box he carried around contained notes for reference, but the really important information was locked away in that safe – and now, apparently, lies with the killer or someone else implicated in either scandal."

Damn! I couldn't catch a break!

"There is one thing I could use your help with," Warren began, "We found a piece of a letter in the box. While it doesn't say much, we want to verify that it was written by Ed's hand.

Would you be able to recognize Ed's handwriting, Donna?"

"Oh sure."

Warren placed a scruffy, ripped piece of paper in front of me. I felt instant sadness. There was no question it had been written by Ed. I nodded and Warren whisked the paper away in a flash.

Before I had a chance to recoup, Peg cleared her throat. Uh oh.

"Detective," Peg began, "if the information isn't all that critical to the case, would it hurt to share some of the details with us?"

"Actually, it would if the information sent you off in a flurry of investigating that could potentially be lethal. Am I accurate in my assumption?"

Peg's facial expression answered Warren's question. So Warren went on.

"This case appears to be far more lethal than either of the other murders you ladies have investigated. Until we know more, we must assume that these murders were not the work of an amateur. It could get real ugly, real fast. And I don't want to dig you out of a commercial dumpster, if you get my point."

That scared us straight. We made our way out of there in record time.

Feeling deflated by Warren's extremely effective scare tactics, we decided to stop at Brick & Mortar for a glass of wine before the drive home. We sat on their cushy leather couches, looking out the large plate glass windows, and at the ultra-modern steel bar and sighed in frustration.

"She's right," Peg began.

"She is," Babs agreed.

I nodded my head. But that didn't stop the feelings of dejection and helplessness over not being able to help find my friend's killer. Cora had been working late, and stopped in to help lift our spirits when we called to tell her things hadn't gone well at the station. She ordered a cup of hot tea with lemon and sat back to hear what had robbed us of our enthusiasm.

As we proceeded to regale her with our frustrations, Peg suddenly developed a smug demeanor. Before I had a chance to dive into the reason, we were distracted by a delivery truck that was obviously making its weekly wine delivery.

"Are you ladies alright for now?" the bartender asked. "I have to get this inventory unloaded and checked in."

We assured him we were fine and he could attend to his other duties and our pity party continued. After several minutes, we noticed that Babs was focused elsewhere. And then it started.

"Hey, you're using the wrong ladder," she began, "I see a taller one at the end of the hallway. That will make things a whole lot easier."

An innocent suggestion made to help make life easier for another. Or so you'd think. Babs had noticed the delivery guy was on a short ladder, hefting cases of wine up onto a high shelf. Naturally, when she noticed a ladder that would make the job considerably less painful – she shared her observation.

"Hey, thanks Lady, you're right," he responded as he climbed the few short steps down from his ladder and dragged the taller, better ladder over to the shelf he was loading. Just as he ascended to the top of the higher ladder with his case of wine, a cry could be heard from the doorway to the supply room.

"Nooooooo!!!!!! That ladder..."

BAM! The warning cry from the now hysterical bartender came a hair too late. Apparently, he had chosen the shorter ladder because the taller one was in need of repair. And now it was kindling. As soon as the delivery man hit the top rung with his case of wine, the entire ladder began to split and splinter. He and his wine case went toppling to the floor, their fall cushioned by three stacked cases of wine below. There began a mad scramble to determine if the rapidly forming burgundy lake was, in fact, comprised of burgundy only or some essential bodily fluids.

Once we were satisfied the delivery guy, whose name was revealed to be Gus, was winded but otherwise unscathed, we cleared out of the bar area to watch the cascading stream of wine and broken glass intertwined with soggy cardboard.

"Uh oh," was all Babs had to say.

Offering to pay for the broken wine was not enough to keep them from tossing us out on our ears. Too bad, it was such a convenient place to grab a glass of wine after a hard day – I doubted we'd be welcomed back anytime soon.

"Hey guys," Peg stopped us mid-step, "Let's stop into the office for a few minutes, there's something I want to share."

Not in the mood for a pep rally, I followed her with mild trepidation.

"It's nice of you to…"

That was as far as I got.

"Don't be so quick to judge, Donna, I think you will want to hear this. You know when you were verifying Ed's handwriting?"

"Yeah," I replied.

"I bet you didn't notice anything that was written in that letter."

"Well no, I was kind of shaken…,"

"I didn't think so. But I wasn't verifying handwriting, so I strained to see whatever I could make out."

"You're kidding," Babs said. "Well, don't keep us in suspense, what did it say?"

"I wasn't able to see much, but I did make out that Ed was telling someone he suspected Ron of theft and fraud. It also said that at least one of the distributors he worked for was thought to be "connected.""

"Like mob connected?" Cora hissed.

"You tell me." Peg responded.

"What kind of theft and fraud?" I asked.

"Something to do with wine tastings was all I could make out."

Holy crap! No wonder Warren was so worried about our involvement. We'd really have to be careful if we decided to move forward. And we'd have to be extremely diligent in considering the safety of anyone else we might choose to involve. It was one thing to throw caution to the wind and press on with the investigation, but it was quite another thing to deliberately involve innocent victims. Oh well, plenty of time to think all that through tomorrow. We'd had quite enough excitement for one day.

[CHAPTER 16]

The next morning, Cora and I reviewed the station visit from the day before so I could bring her fully up-to-speed. We also agreed that we were likely to be persona non grata at Brick & Mortar. It took a full minute after our reminiscence to determine a next step in moving this investigation into high gear, responsibly.

"Don't you Google everything?" she asked.

She was right. The first step would normally have been to compile a list of names with a known or suspected connection to the case and search for them online. Further proof that these times were anything but normal. In our case, less hands on meant more life expectancy.

We spent ten minutes coming up with a workable list. I agreed to contact Abby and see if we were missing any key names. Then I would research them online and start to build profiles of our cast of characters. I could do that over lunch.

Then we spent another ten minutes discussing how Cora would approach the various financial aspects of the case. She would build scenarios for Ron's nefarious activities and speculate on how each one would effect the other parties involved. This exercise would be aided enormously by my conversation with Abby.

In addition to running financial scenarios on our case, Cora would also run similar assumptions on Liv and Maxie's case. Our goal was to divide and conquer, but we would share all the available resources – Cora was unquestionably a resource from a financial standpoint.

When all was said and done, we figured it would take a few days for each of us to complete our assignments. Ideally, we'd regroup before the weekend.

* * *

I left a message on Abby's voicemail and checked my email.

Engrossed in media research, I was startled by the ringing of the phone. Glancing at the ID window on the phone, I saw that it was Abby.

"Hey Abby, how are you doing?"

"I have good and bad moments. You know Ed would never have wanted us to spend time grieving. He would have been all about hustling to promote his saint-like memory."

"So true, Abby. Glad to hear your sense of humor has not deserted you."

I proceeded to fill Abby in on the periphery of the case with Ron. She had been aware that her Dad had been recruited as a kind of "wine detective" on a dozen or so cases over the years, but she was not aware of the specifics of the case against Ron. I gave her just enough information to understand the need to share the names of related parties, without giving her the desire to go out and conduct her own investigation – or so I hoped.

By the time our call was complete, I had the names of several of the folks closest to Ron, and a clear path for my investigation. I gave my best to Abby and her Mom and said my goodbyes.

Normally, I would attempt to interview anyone I felt the need to investigate. But these folks would have to be hyper-researched. I could not take the chance that a mob connection could make a few seemingly innocent questions my entre into the Missouri with cement shoes.

In my conversation with Abby, I outlined some of the various scenarios that Cora felt could build wealth quickly for a man in Ron's position. Related to the wine tastings themselves were his bosses at all the wineries – and there were several. He conducted wine tastings for a few of the well-known California houses, Bartoni, generally considered a pedestrian table wine, the Bartoni vineyards also produced a little known fine wine; the house of Schroeder, a big bold selection of reds with some oaky and forgettable whites; Camerotti, owned by the famous Italian actor Vincenzo Camerotti who made a wine ideally suited for removing rust from old nails (and who couldn't keep said wine in stock along with his various and sundry other promotional items), and finally, Flowering Rosemary, a relatively new house connected to the Culinary Institute. These wines were created to pair with their specialty dishes. The focus was more on the food, and the wines were heavily laced with herbs and, in some cases, orchard fruits.

Abby also gave me the names of some of Ron's key connections at these wineries. At this point, I had a burgeoning list of suspects. I asked Abby if any rose to the surface as being particularly volatile.

"Camerotti is quite a character. There have been rumors of mob connections for years, but I don't see him as much of a threat since this wine business was started as a lark and has earned him far more than he could imagine in his wildest dreams," she offered.

"But don't those people have overinflated egos that become outraged when they're not treated like the royalty they believe themselves to be?" Here I was using Donny as my example of self-adoration.

"I suppose, I hadn't thought of it quite in that way," she acknowledged. "Schroeder is a big, loving, happy family. They all work together, they all love their wine and their family. I can't imagine them treating any form of duplicity with much more than a stern show of disappointment."

"Do you know much about how the family runs? Or who's calling the shots?"

"Well, now that you mention it, there were rumors of a falling out several years ago. One brother was determined to appoint himself head, and that's just not how things had been done up to that point. For years, there was collaboration and agreement. You know, I wasn't interested enough to find out how things netted out after that. If that brother got his way, it's possible the Schroeder family has become a bit more aggressive in how they protect their interests."

As we continued to review the folks at each location, it became increasingly clear that, for one quirky reason or another, no one could be ruled out. I was getting tired just thinking of all the research. I was also getting itchy. Despite the warning signs, I was used to getting out and talking to folks to build my case. Lucky for me, I had Cora to keep me grounded and stop me from doing anything really stupid – too soon.

After talking to Abby I was anxious to get started investigating Ron's bosses. I wanted to review all the facts with Cora so we could map out a strategy. I also wanted to ensure that I had a clear end in sight and wasn't just spinning my wheels.

Together, we decided that talking to the folks at these wineries was risky, but not impossible. We felt the main goal would be to determine whether or not any of them was onto Ron and his thievery. It might even make sense to dig a little deeper to see if any of the vineyard employees might be in on these scams with Ron.

We came up with a positively brilliant approach. I would call each vineyard, ask for one of the key people Abby had identified and tell them I'd been at one of Ron's recent tastings. I would go on to explain that Ron had provided some interesting details about their winery and I wanted to be sure to capture all of the salient data so I could host my own private little wine tasting at home.

We figured this approach would keep any suspicion off of me, and would at least let us know whether or not Ron was still affiliated with that particular winery. If it turned out he'd been dismissed, it was likely they had been onto him, and that would have made Ed's investigation a lot more dangerous for Ron and could have been the cause of Ed's death. We would have to tread lightly.

It was imperative that I have my questions lined up so I wouldn't flub the interview and cast suspicion on myself. It was also imperative that I have some notion of what I was really looking to uncover. I honestly didn't know how Ron could manage to amass a small fortune off of a handful of wineries. That's where Cora was so invaluable. She had spent a few hours researching the wine industry and she had some theories on how fraud could most easily and most profitably be perpetrated.

"First, there's wine headed to a tasting that never makes it to the table," she began.

"You mean like something is wrong with it?"

"Yes, either the bottle is broken in transit or the wine, when opened, is found to be corked," she continued.

"But how would that put money in Ron's pocket?"

"Those bottles wouldn't really be broken or corked, and

Ron would sell them on the side," she replied.

"How often could he get away with something like that?" I asked.

"More often than you might think. Especially since he was dealing with four major and a handful of minor wineries. A lot of bottles were passing through Ron's possession."

This seemed like a good place to start. Once we wrote our list of questions, I felt ready to hit the phones. Cora managed to throw cold water all over that idea.

"What happened to all of that research you were going to do?"

"Well, do I really need research now that we have a solid game plan for actually investigating?"

"I think you do. Whatever you can learn about these wineries and the individuals can only make you more prepared and make your call seem more credible."

I had to give her that. So I spent the next few hours conducting an online review of anything and everything I could find about the wineries and the people I would try to call. And actually, Cora was right again. Expecting to find little more than boring vineyard stats and standard bios in my search, I was pleasantly surprised to find that each of the major vineyards had a fair amount of press, not all of which was positive. One or two of the really smaller vineyards had bad news that ended in prison or bankruptcy. Who knew this was where the excitement would lie?

At least I was forearmed going in. I decided I'd prepped

enough and it was time to take action. My first call was to the good old family folks at Schroeder. There was nothing horrific in my scan of the winery. Just a wholesome, clean cut family who loved to work together on making quality wines. The worst thing I read about them was that Grandma Schroeder gave a wine critic the raspberry when he panned their best effort in white wine. I didn't feel too threatened by their history, so it seemed like a good place to start.

"Schroeder vineyards, how may I help you?"

"Hello, may I speak with Tiffany Schroeder?" I asked. I knew she was one of the younger family members and their head of marketing.

"This is Tiffany," came a cheery, girlish voice.

"Tiffany, my name is Belinda Weatherby, how are you today?" I asked.

"Just fine, Ms. Weatherby, how may I help you on this lovely day?"

"I was recently at one of your wine tastings. A tasting conducted by a gentleman named Ron something or other."

"Oh yes, that would be Ron Menlow, he's one of our most productive distributors. I certainly hope you enjoyed your experience, Ma'am."

"Why yes, Tiffany. In fact, so much so that I was hoping to find when Ron would be conducting some other tastings in the MidWest. I have many friends in the area who would like to experience him first hand."

"I'm so pleased to hear that Ms. Weatherby. If you'll just

give me your email address, I'll be happy to send you Ron's schedule for the next two months..."

"Oh, you kids and those new-fangled contraptions. I never did get one of those fancy computers, but if I give you a fax number..."

"Of course Ms. Weatherby, I'll be happy to fax you the schedule." Whew, that was close. I'd have to remember not to ask for any written data if I wanted to keep my identity somewhat of a secret. That was a huge problem in this day and age – stealth was a thing of the past and it was way too easy to be tracked down. Even giving her a fax number was a risk, but I had no reason to believe she would try to find me based on our extremely innocuous conversation.

I had learned one critical thing from this call, Ron was still on fairly good terms with Schroeder. Tiffany wasn't at all hesitant in proclaiming their admiration of Ron. She would not likely have reacted in that way if they'd begun to suspect that Ron was defrauding them in any way.

I called several more vineyards with a similar reaction until I finally hit paydirt. When I called Bartoni and asked for Gianni Verdino, things could not have been more different.

"Hello, Mr. Verdino, this is Belinda Weatherby."

"Yes, Ms. Weatherby, what can I do for you?"

I proceeded to go through my Ron story as I had with all the others. Gianni Verdino's reaction, however, was not at all the same.

"I'm sorry, Madam, there is no one of that name in our

employ at this time," came his rather curt reply.

"Oh well, could I have possibly gotten the name wrong?" I used the daffy old geezer approach in an effort to dig a little deeper. No soap.

"Madam, I am afraid you are mistaken about your encounter with our brand. Now, I am in rather a hurry and must respectfully take my leave."

His leave didn't feel all that respectful. But I knew where the sore spot lie. It was clear that Ron had lost his lucrative position with Bartoni fairly recently. It seemed too much of a coincidence that his removal from the company came from any other source than Ed's investigation. In my eyes, Verdino shot to the head of the list of suspects. I also had to wonder, was there an insider at Bartoni that had also profited from Ron's nefarious scheme? If so, it would have magnified the danger to Ed. And to anyone trying to avenge his death.

If we find a friendly source within the Bartoni organization to give us a little insight into just what exactly Ron had been up to and what they proposed to do about it – that would help to determine the scope of the issue. I also wondered if someone at Bartoni was likely to contact Ron's other wineries to warn them. That would be a lot more difficult and put us/me much closer to risk. As I contemplated this problem, Maxie called to say that we were all meeting for coffee in the morning, and an update on our progress. I was anxious to share my progress and get their assessment of next steps. It would take all the resources of our think tank to arrive at the next best course of action. And, in retrospect, I had to wonder how unbelievably stupid Ron was in pitting himself against multiple adversaries, some of whom were connected up the wazoo.

[CHAPTER 17]

Later that night, Jon and I enjoyed a lovely home cooked meal with champagne. No special occasion, we've just learned that creating special occasions to treat ourselves is a lot more rewarding than waiting around and letting the calendar dictate what days should be special or not.

Over a fine selection by Mumm and lovely escargot with parsley and garlic butter prepared by Jon, we discussed Ron and his dubious activities. Once I had briefed Jon on all we'd found and where we felt the investigation should go next, he was quick to both congratulate and caution me.

"You got some great information and I know Warren will be grateful for your intelligence. But, I think this is where your investigation has to end."

"But Jon,"

"Do you know the Bartoni's have a nickname in the industry?"

"No." My knowledge of wine-related facts paled miserably in comparison to Jon's. He seemed to learn and retain volumes of fascinating facts relating to all aspects of the business. I was more than a little jealous because it often made him the center of attention at our frequent social gatherings. Yes, I know that's small and petty, I'm working on it.

"Bartoni sono deadly."

I gulped.

"That's right. They are notorious for their mob connections. In fact, they are the ruling family on the west coast."

"But wouldn't we be helping them?"

"Do you think they need or want your help?"

He had a point. Never had I read of a mob family welcoming outside help from an ad agency in finding and dealing with someone who had cheated them.

"What the hell is wrong with Ron?"

"Ah, that's the $64,000 question," Jon replied. "Was Ron just a guy who got so cocky he thought he was invincible?"

"That would be nothing short of suicide."

"It would. But I don't think that's what happened here. I remember reading something about the Bartoni family, and an east coast branch that became estranged from them when the rest made their way from Philly to wine country in order to become vintners. It was an obscure and well-kept secret, but that branch of the family relocated to Cincinnati in order to completely disassociate themselves from the gangsters that all moved west."

"I'm not sure where you're going with all this."

"I also read, at a much later time, that Ron had hailed from Cincinnati. It seems just too much of a coincidence."

"So you think..."

"That Ron is a descendant of the Bartoni family from Cincinnati. Yes, that's precisely what I think. And I think he's a greedy, hotheaded little punk who didn't want his distant relatives to be the only ones to make money off of California grapes."

"Wow, that's amazing Jon. You may have wrapped this whole case up for Warren," I gushed.

"Well, its educated guessing, but it's still just guessing," Jon shrugged.

"But there is one other related guess that is possibly the most critical of all."

"Yeah? What?"

"I also think that cousin Ron has managed to collect some gangster friends himself. And that's why further investigating on your part will be suicide just as much as it was for Ed."

That was undoubtedly a sobering thought. Suddenly the champagne was less festive and the escargot were less succulent – all I could taste was sawdust as I considered Jon's assumptions. I had no intention of being one of those amateur sleuths who laughed in the face of certain and impending danger. My biggest concern, at the moment, was in whether or not I had already set into motion a chain of events that could get me and my think tank killed. Clearly we'd have a somber coffee klatch in the morning.

* * *

We all arrived at Aroma's at about the same time. That was good, I could dive right into my concerns and not have to repeat myself. Once I outlined Jon's assessment, there was dead silence.

Maxie was the first to respond. "So you're on to the next logical step."

I picked up on her line of thought. "Yes, Jon and I have good friends in Cincinnati. Well, actually, just over the border into Kentucky. Billy and Rosella know the Cincinnati market inside out. They know the players. We'll call them tonight and brief them on how they can help us sift through the Cincinnati Bartonis."

"But won't that put them at risk?" Liv was always the pragmatic one.

"They're insiders," I replied, "they know which bricks to kick and which to avoid. And they have family throughout the city who are involved in just about every industry you could imagine all told. For all I know, they already have all the answers we seek. They just don't know we need them."

I wasn't quite as optimistic as I sounded, but for the first time I felt as though the brakes were off and we could really make some headway in this investigation. I made a mental note to Skype Jon later and fill him in on our new plans for the evening. Jon always enjoyed chatting with our Kentucky friends. Billy and Jon had gone to school together in upstate New York way back in high school. Billy had a sharp and caustic sense of humor that never failed to make us laugh.

His observations about life were not far behind those of George Carlin. And his lovely southern wife, Rosella, had a gentle way of laying the final brick to his diatribes in a seemingly effortless manner. The two were like a traveling comedy show for folks with a penchant for sophisticated humor.

Ironically, it had not occurred to me to involve Billy and Rosella until Maxie had pronounced her one simple statement. I had to wonder if she had some sort of gift for telepathy. She didn't even have to say the words to put me on the right track. And that happened on a fairly regular basis. A simple pronouncement from her and my thoughts became focused and directed. Working with her had been really good for me. I just hoped she had that same effect on everyone – our productivity would be through the roof!

Knowing that the Bartoni side of the investigation would be well underway after tonight, I decided to focus on another leg of inquiry. Any good investigator knows you can't rule anything out even if you think you're heading down the right path. It's always best to pursue multiple avenues of exploration so you don't lose valuable time if you hit a dead end on any one of them.

I was thinking perhaps the Schroeder brothers deserved a second look while Billy and Rosella were in hot pursue of the less successful branch of the Bartoni clan. Before I had a chance to formulate an approach for Schroeder, Liv got my attention.

"Our investigation is not so far along," she admitted. "We hit a snag when our craft brewery client had a major emergency."

I knew about this incident, but not all the gory details. She proceeded to tell us about a new, dark Belgium-style beer that fizzed itself right up and out of the vats just before its promotional event was being finalized.

"Yeah," Maxie concurred, "we had all hands on deck, calling to cancel everything from the ads to the venue, the caterer and all of the entertainment. It was pretty devastating."

After taking several minutes to discuss this major setback for our client, and all of the implications, Cora took the lead in helping us get past the problem and move on to the investigation.

"It's just as well," she started, "I've had a chance to build you some financial what ifs that will help to focus your line of inquiry."

She proceeded to lay out her various hypotheses as we listened with rapt attention. The best part of Cora's analysis was that it shone a direct light on four specific individuals. Researching those four would be the logical starting point. Liv agreed to do a thorough online search and Maxie would begin by contacting her wine-industry connections for any indication of dubious behavior on the part of any one of the four. Based on their enthusiasm I figured they'd be up-to-speed within 24-hours.

We finished up and headed into the office.

[CHAPTER 18]

That night, Jon and I had our conversation with Billy and Rosella. They were amazing. Not only did they know of the Bartoni family and the fact they that had split into the Cincinnati side and the Napa side, they also knew every one of the Cincinnati family members, as well as all of the history and rumors.

"Yes, Rosella assured us, "Ron Menlow was a distant cousin of the Bartoni's. His father married one of the Capilla girls and her mother had been a Bartoni. I know a lot about Ron because we went to junior high together."

I could not believe my luck. Rosella actually knew Ron personally, and she confirmed everything Jon had suspected, except the bitterness over the success of the Napa side of the family. But she did confirm that Ron had been a hothead who was always looking for a fight. He was also very protective of his mother. He seemed to believe she had been dealt some dirty blows in her early life – and his own father had not exactly been the ideal husband.

When you added those facts up, it was not difficult to believe that Ron might have set his sites on getting even with the successful, wine-making side of his mother's family.

Especially since we knew, for sure, that his entire career had been in the wine industry. It seemed too much of a coincidence, Ron had somehow become involved in an industry in which a remote group of relatives, with whom he had no contact, were major players.

But, would his bitterness and need to make his family pay for his Mother's difficult life give him enough reason to feel compelled to commit murder? That did seem like a bit of a stretch. Even if his family had mob connections, would Billy's bad boy behavior really put him in enough danger to warrant the murder of someone who seemed about to expose him?

As excited as I'd become during our conversation, that thought threw some cold water on my buzz. It was imperative that I continue to pursue all avenues, no matter how perfect a solution Ron's dilemma seemed to present.

Billy and Rosella went on to profile Bartoni family members scattered throughout the Cincinnati area. During the course of our conversation, they prepared a short list of folks they could interview to get more in-depth on Ron's adult persona. Rosella felt that, if Ron's penchant for rough play had expanded as he aged, it could be possible he would whack someone almost for the pure sport of it. That was a concept I had not yet entertained. I felt as though our friends had an excellent handle on their segment of the investigation.

After our talk of wine careers and murder, we chatted about their three kids and the whole extended family. Then we moved on to their next visit to Omaha and agreed to get it scheduled within the next few weeks. It had been far too long since we'd had a chance to sit down face-to-face and enjoy our friendship. But you know that old and tired saying, life just gets in the way.

Once off the phone, Jon and I spent the next hour or so reviewing everything I knew and everything we suspected. We took careful notes so we didn't lose any of the threads that needed pursuing.

Jon was showing more of an interest in the actual investigating than usual. Generally, at this point in an investigation, he has already written down his suspect and placed it in an envelope inside of a book. And he's two for two. For some reason, this investigation had him more stumped. And it was clearly bugging him. I saw it as an opportunity to get him actively involved. I was certain he'd enjoy the process, and I knew I'd feel safer if he was working side-by-side with me.

It seemed as though he could jump in on the Flowering Rosemary side. As an exceptional chef and something of a wine connoisseur – although he'd humbly deny both – I felt he would be the ideal sleuth for the folks at the Culinary Institute. And I was certain, knowing his chilling accuracy, that they wouldn't know what hit them.

Once I subtly suggested that Jon take this on, he virtually leapt into action. For the next hour, he hugged his keyboard while his fingers flew in all directions.

I used this opportunity to scrutinize everything we had

done and were planning to do. We were covering a lot of ground, but were we correct in assuming that Ed's demise was tied to one of his two current investigations? After all, he had been called into action in pursuit of others over the years. Might one of them have suddenly developed a reason, or the opportunity to get back at him for perceived past wrongs? Or was it something outside of the wine industry altogether?

As much as I hated to bother her, I felt it was necessary to spend some time with Eva and debrief her on all the rest of the aspects of Ed's life. I felt that the wine crimes were in good hands what with Jon on Flowering Rosemary, Billy and Rosella on Bartoni and Maxie and Liv on Cal's investment concerns, I could take a break and look at something completely outside of that focus.

I made a call to Eva.

"I am so sorry to bother you, Sweetie, I know it's a really really bad time, but I hope you understand that I would never forgive myself if I didn't help get to the bottom of exactly what happened to Ed."

"Oh Donna, I do so appreciate how you feel," Eva responded, "but I think it would be healthier for you, and certainly safer, if you would just drop this whole thing. While I appreciate your determination to investigate Ed's cases and carry on his good work, I know there's a part of you that thinks you're solving Ed's murder, and as I've told you before, he was not murdered."

I did not expect that. I figured Eva would be weepy and might not feel up to exploring and examining old memories, but not that she would still be so clearly in denial and would try to stop me from doing whatever possible to find Ed's killer. I appreciated her concern for my safety and well-being. Maybe if I tried again.

"I just can't rest until we get some answers."

"Look Donna," she replied, "the police are making some good progress on both of the investigations Ed was conducting. We know a few extremely dangerous individuals are involved in each of the cases. Please do not make me worry about you on top of everything else I'm dealing with now."

Oh man, that got to me. Was I being selfish here? I was so quick to criticize Clovis' selfishness and maybe I was doing the very same thing I accused her of, putting my needs above everything else. That gave me pause for thought.

But the more I thought, the more I came back to one puzzling aspect. No matter how hard I tried, I could not get a tone of anything but nervousness out of all of Eva's comments. No deep and heart-wrenching sorrow. No unending grief. How could that be? Eva and Ed were closer than any couple I knew. How could she not be grief-stricken? At first I thought her nervousness was a fear that the killer might want to kill her as well – which would certainly be understandable. But, if I was any judge of human nature – I didn't think it was fear-based nervousness. In fact, it sounded just like someone trying to get me the hell off the phone.

Now there are those who would understand perfectly why someone would be in a rush to get off the phone with me. In fact, Ed could have waxed philosophic for hours on the benefits of doing that. But not Eva. Something wasn't right. As she continued to nervously try to dissuade me from pursuing the investigation, or even talking about it for that matter, a horrible thought struck me.

Could Eva possibly have been involved in Ed's murder? I quickly dismissed that possibility. It's not like I could voice that thought with anyone I knew – they'd all think I was mad. But when I reviewed our conversation in my head, there it was, nervousness and guilt.

Try as I might, I could not get that thought to stop popping into my brain. I could feel myself starting to panic. The mere concept that Eva could have some involvement was pure insanity – but why else would she feel guilt. At that moment, I knew I had to do two things, first, get Eva to agree to meet in person. I had to see her reactions for myself. And second, think this through and try to understand how or why guilt on Eva's behalf might enter into the picture.

"Eva," I began. "If it makes you uncomfortable for me to pursue this, I'll quit."

"You will, Donna?" There was a palpable note of doubt.

"Of course I will. You have to know that my first priority is to help you and Abby in any way possible. If my sleuthing is giving you the least little bit of agita, I'll stop immediately."

I think she bought it. I heard a sigh. So I pressed on.

"But you have to agree to have lunch with me tomorrow."

"Well, this week is a little difficult..."

"No Eva, no excuses. You have to let me help somehow."

"Well, alright, I suppose..."

"Good, we'll meet at the French Bakery in LaVista at noon."

She agreed and we signed off. This was a turn in my investigation that I did not expect. But I felt it was a necessary avenue to pursue. Then I directed my energy toward thoughts on why Eva might possibly be feeling guilt. Had she encouraged him to pursue an investigation against his will? I quickly ruled that out. Anyone who knew Ed, knew he did what he wanted. I then wondered if she'd suggested a line of pursuit that was particularly dangerous – that seemed more likely – but it was still a longshot. After about an hour of cogitation, I came to the conclusion that it was conceivable that Eva might just feel guilt at Ed's demise, albeit indirectly and undoubtedly unwarranted.

That's when I realized that tomorrow's lunch would likely be more about two friends trying to help each other through a difficult period than about an investigation. I would try to focus on the cause of Eva's guilt and persuade her that it was pointless and unnecessary. If I could do that, I would genuinely be doing some good. And after all, wasn't that the point of everything?

[CHAPTER 19]

The morning started off with two fire drills. Once resolved, they hardly seemed worth the energy, but in the throes
of the moment, we were fighting for our lives. One client had
been notified that the invitations for their upcoming event
had been shipped to their St. Louis office instead of to
Omaha. That proved to be a false report, the invitations
were already sitting on their Omaha loading dock. Another
client had been told by a neighbor that their TV spot had
been interrupted by a competitor's spot. We never found out
what that neighbor was smoking, but we were able to assure
the client that no such mistake had occurred. Well-meaning
people often sound well-meaning, but completely misplaced
alarm – and we're off to the races to set things straight.

By the time everything was resolved and everyone involved was once again happy, my adrenalin was starting to
drain. Rather than wait for the inevitable adrenalin crash,
I grabbed my purse and headed out to the bakery lunch
with Eva a little on the early side.

I didn't know the staff at the LaVista bakery as well as I
knew that of its sister business, Le Voltaire, or the original
French bakery next door. I grabbed a table in the corner

and perused the menu while waiting for Eva's arrival. True to her word, she arrived promptly. After a tearful hug we settled in and placed our orders. Croque madam was the perfect comfort food for this day, when the clouds in the sky were a fitting match for our heavy hearts.

For the first fifteen minutes, we discussed what life was like these days for Eva and Abby. I asked a series of questions in what I thought was a caring and gentle way, and Eva continued in her pattern of nervous guilt. It was driving me crazy. I finally hit the breaking point and as typical of my style – I jumped right in with both feet.

"Am I reading you right? Is it possible you're feeling guilt?"

Before responding I could see a clear "deer in the headlights" look on Eva's face. This woman should never play poker. After what seemed an eternity, she began a halting explanation.

"I, I do feel guilty."

"What on earth for?" Never one to be subtle, but I just knew there could be nothing nefarious behind Eva's odd countenance, and I had to get to the bottom of it.

"Well, you, and the others."

"What about me and what others?"

"All of our wonderful friends, trying so hard to help, and in your case putting yourself in harm's way."

"And that makes you feel guilty?"

She nodded.

"But you didn't ask anyone..."

"I know, Donna, but I've been so worried about Ed for such a long time. I just knew something horrific would happen to him. He was playing with fire. And I was right. I just couldn't bear it if something were to happen to you or Jon or any of our friends because of the hideous thing that happened to Ed."

All of this made sense, sort of. I just couldn't help but feel that Eva did not deliver this message in a terribly convincing manner. And I was starting to feel guilty about my suspicions. Sitting with Eva did, however, allay any fears that she could possibly be involved in Ed's demise in any way. She was the picture of innocence – and a terrible actress.

"Are you sure that's all it is?"

"Well, there is a part of me that feels guilty for encouraging Ed to help his friends out and embark on those dangerous investigations. I should have known there was potential danger, but I had this image of Ed as Robin Hood, helping the poor honest folks who were victimized by this continual string of sleazy characters."

Now that made more sense, and sounded far more credible. But the thought of Ed as Robin Hood was a little hard to swallow. I did have to stifle a chuckle at the thought of him in green tights and a pointy hat. Sadly, I would not have the opportunity to bust his chops about that visual image – at least not in this lifetime.

I assured Eva that nothing any of us would do would

place us directly in harm's way. In fact, I shared some of our frustration at having to proceed so cautiously because of the inherent danger in being around some of these shady characters. She seemed a bit more at ease after I outlined our "safety first" process. But just a bit.

"So Eva, how comfortable would you be in reviewing some of the other aspects of Ed's life with me – so we can rule out other possibilities?"

"Sure, I guess we could do that."

So we spent the next hour and a half discussing virtually every aspect of Ed's life. Even those occurring before he met Eva. I felt it was a worthwhile exercise in that it effectively ruled out any other possibility aside from one of the investigations. In retrospect, there might have been a teacher or two who would have gladly kicked him in the butt, but not murder.

After we had reviewed Ed's childhood and early life, we began to review the investigations that Ed had pursued and resolved before the time of his death. There were two that probably warranted further investigation. Eva thought in one case the miscreant might have since died, and in the other the suspect turned out to be creepy, but innocent. So I didn't think it would take long to wrap up everything save for the two open investigations at the time of Ed's death.

I did notice that, although Eva seemed less jumpy, she never lost that nervous darting eye movement. Just as we were wrapping up our lunch meeting, the door opened and in walked Nic from Le Voltaire. I could have sworn he saw us, yet he quickly walked past our table and into the kitchen with an armload of bread. I figured he'd be back out to chat in just a moment, but I was wrong. I wanted to greet him before leaving, so I asked the young girl at the counter to tell him we wanted to say hi.

She was back in a moment with apologies. He thought he'd noticed us on his way in, but fear of dropping baguettes made him hustle directly into the kitchen. And now there was a problem with some piece of equipment. It was making quite a mess and he couldn't step away for even a moment. That was odd. Nic had never struck me as the mechanical type, but I suppose working in a commercial kitchen makes one resourceful.

Eva and I hugged and parted. On my way back to the office it dawned on me, I was suspecting everyone of something. If I couldn't quell this hyper sensitivity I wouldn't be able to spot a real clue if it came up and bit me in the face.

A lot of amateur sleuthing has more to do with controlling one's own innate tendencies enough to be able to let the intuitive side search for the truth. Being overeager was not a plus, but rather a huge distraction. I guess not being able to get out and talk to everyone involved was taking a toll on my sensing ability. I wondered if I'd be at all useful if I couldn't keep it under wraps. Maybe I was just too close to it. I had to admit to myself that the whole sleuthing gig was considerably less enjoyable when the victim was someone that mattered to you. You could be so much more objective when you weren't also feeling grief.

* * *

Back at the office, I spent about forty-five minutes researching the two closed investigations. Eva was right, the one guy had died two years prior. The other guy, the one who was exonerated, had gone on to great fortune and was currently living the good life on his private island in the Maldives. It was a soft but firm close to both of those doors. I mean, someone related to one of the cases could be taking revenge on their behalf – but that seemed like way too much of a stretch. So it was back to handling Ron's case. I needed to talk to those Schroeder brothers, tout de suite.

I placed a call to the Schroeder empire and was told that someone would get back to me ASAP.

[CHAPTER 20]

Tiffany called me back at just about 5:15.

"I'm sorry it took me so long Ms. Weatherby. Was Ron not able to help you with your private wine tasting?"

Did I detect the slightest note of annoyance in the little Barbie doll's voice? How do you like that? All that sunshine in paradise and she cracks as the slightest of inconveniences.

"Oh my dear, I'm terribly sorry to disturb you," I began. "I've been thinking about my wine tasting and you see, it will also be an important fund raising event for my favorite charity, so I want to ensure that I can draw only the most prominent and generous of Omaha's philanthropists, and to do that, one's event must be top notch as well as mutli-faceted."

"Of course, Ms. Weatherby, I didn't realize. How may I help?" asked a suitably contrite Tiffany.

"Well my dear," I went on, "you know some of the major donors are getting up there in age, and many don't get around all that much."

"I see."

"And well, you know, the more exciting we can make an event, the more chance we'll intrigue them enough to want to come, and the more interesting and enjoyable the event the more charitable they tend to feel."

"And just how do you expect me to help you with that, Ms. Weatherby?"

"Well, Tiffany, I was at a particularly successful event last summer and I thought I'd take a page from their book."

"Do tell."

"The event was an art festival of sorts. The potential patrons were invited to view and hopefully purchase the art. Donations were solicited to support the organization that housed the artists and their workshops."

"Ms. Weatherby, I don't think I understand..."

"Give me a chance to explain, dear. As much as was possible, we shared stories of the artists themselves. We tried to paint as complete a picture in order to make the patrons feel a connection. What we found was that the more exciting and exotic the artists' stories, the more the patrons wanted to pour money into the cause."

"I still don't see how..."

"I was hoping you might have some juicy family stories that I could share with my..."

"Oh, no. No, no, no. I can assure you, Ms. Weatherby, that the Schroeder family is absolutely and completely boringly vanilla. There is just nothing there that would titillate or even interest..."

"Not even that little tiff among your brothers?"

"Now just one minute, how could you possibly..."

"It doesn't matter how I know, Tiffany. What matters is how I can get enough details to intrigue my monied guests."

To my great surprise, not to mention irritation, Tiffany began to cry. Oh crap, I did not see that coming. One might say I had gone too far – again.

"Oh my dear, I am so sorry to bring up bad memories," I began at somewhat of a loss.

"It's not that," Tiffany sniffled, "I just had no idea that word of our troubles had leaked out to the general population. We thought we'd kept the whole thing under wraps."

"I don't think the general population is aware, Tiffany. I just happen to be connected to a lot of folks inside the wine industry. You can't be surprised that those folks have an inkling of the dissention within your ranks, can you?"

"I suppose not, I suppose we've all just been kidding ourselves. Hans and Wolfie have not exactly been discreet in their efforts to garner support for themselves. They are such meatheads!"

"Boys will be boys."

That sounded lame even to me.

"That is so true, Ms. Weatherby. They are just stupid boys who don't understand the consequences of their childish and selfish actions. It is clear that we will have to deal more severely with the boys."

Holy cow! My image of sweet little Tiffany suddenly reverted to a Frau Bleuker-like countenance. And did I hear just the slightest German inflection? I began to think I was dealing with the true power behind the Schroeder empire.

"Alright, I'll give you some interesting information for your charity event."

Now I was starting to sweat a little. I didn't like her tone – at all.

"Well Tiffany, if this makes you uncomfortable..." I started to backtrack.

"No, Ms. Weatherby, you wanted a titillating story for your guests, and I will give you just that."

There was nothing for it but to sit tight and keep my mouth shut. This was Tiffany's show. But I was starting to wonder how Ron could possibly even fit into the equation at all. Tiffany's story would focus on her brothers. Would there be a way for me to pull Ron into her painful tale? As it turned out, I didn't have long to wonder.

"It all started..."

Tiffany went on to regale me with the story of an idyllic childhood. She and her brothers were very close and they shared wonderful hours of playing among the vineyards and among the nearby fruit orchard. Their parents encouraged their blissful play, but also taught them the necessary lessons of responsibility that would be necessary for them to succeed in running the entire wine empire. As was the custom with so many families of European origin the eldest son, Hans, was destined to be the king of that empire. Tiffany and Wolfie were groomed in their respective positions – and they were all happy just to have the privilege of continuing the family legacy.

Everyone knew their place, and there were no surprises.

At this point, Tiffany took a moment. She sighed sorrowfully and went on. Hans wasn't the great leader the family had hoped he'd be. He was more interested in painting the vines than cultivating and harvesting them. Together, Wolfie and I covered for him, as any good family member would. This went on for nearly a decade, and then we hired Ron to do some of our wine tastings.

Oh god, I hadn't expected her story to lead us to Ron quite so neatly. This was starting to get interesting.

Tiffany went on to explain that as Ron became a more integral part of the organization, he could not help but see the discrepancies in the siblings' respective roles. And he couldn't leave it alone. Ron started to invite Wolfie out to party when he was in town. This opened up a whole new world for Wolfie. He had always been very quiet and kept close to home.

Ron had quite the way with the ladies, so he and Wolfie began to be known as the most eligible bachelors in Napa. That wouldn't have been so bad, but in order to pick up some of the more elusive of the women, Ron started telling them that Wolfie was the head of the entire Schroeder family. At first this made Wolfie extremely uncomfortable and he would correct Ron. But soon, Wolfie began to see the difference in female attention. All the girls wanted to be with the head of Schroeder, but not necessarily the head of operations at Schroeder.

Ron could see that Wolfie was extremely disappointed over a life that had formerly seemed like perfection to him. And Ron, a consummate manipulator, saw a way to turn the situation into an advantage for himself.

At this stage, I felt my pulse quicken. Did this mean that Tiffany knew the full extent of Ron's deception? I had to keep my mouth shut and let her continue.

"I'm sorry to say, Ms. Weatherby, that Ron is not the most forthright and upstanding of individuals. I hope you'll be able to see that Ron does not represent the rest of the Schroeder family and staff."

"Oh it never occurred to me that you and your family are anything less than completely upstanding."

"That's a huge relief. While I admit he's a damn good salesman and has increased our sales admirably, I've been getting ready to sack Ron for his ability to create chaos among our staff and our family. Unfortunately, Wolfie still doesn't see it my way, and Hans is virtually worthless when it comes to problem issues with employees. The boys tend to take everyone at face value."

"They don't have your keen ability to see the true motives of outsiders, do they?"

"No they don't, Ms. Weatherby. In fact, they would believe the story you told me when you called today."

"Uh oh, you're not buying it?"

"I wasn't born yesterday, Ms. Weatherby. If that IS in fact your name."

"Well, you really are insightful, aren't you Tiffany?"

"Can the compliments, lady. You want your story and you'll get it. I can only hope that you're as honorable as I read you to be and you don't use this information to hurt Schroeder or anyone else."

Wow, Tiffany was extremely impressive. I no longer had any doubt as to who held the reins at Schroeder, and she deserved to be the power behind the throne. This was one sharp lady.

Tiffany finished her story by describing the gargantuan rift Ron caused between her two brothers. She speculated that Ron had planned to convince Wolfie to overthrow Hans and take over the helm of the company. She thought he would expect special favors as the drinking buddy of the big guy.

I contemplated whether or not to share another theory – that Ron wanted Wolfie in power so that he'd look the other way and allow Ron to pilfer from the company. Plus, with Wolfie at the helm, Tiffany might back off some of the management, and Ron knew that she was the only sibling smart enough to smoke him out. I thought better of going down this road. Tiffany was already getting rid of Ron, so what would be the purpose of adding to her pain and frustration with her brothers. And who knows, maybe she did know and elected to keep the truly illegal stories to herself. I'd allow her that subterfuge.

All of this lead me to believe that the Schroeder situation

could indeed be a reason why Ron might want to kill Ed, if Ed were about to blow the whistle on this sweet gig that Ron had worked so hard to finagle. I thanked Tiffany and swore not to use the information she had shared to harm Schroeder in any way.

I felt this was an avenue worth pursuing. If only I had seen those stolen papers!

[CHAPTER 21]

Driving home that night, I was anxious to share all of my latest findings with Jon. Upon arrival I was somewhat distracted, first by the onslaught of bulldog greetings which rose to a deafening pitch as each one pushed the other away in an effort to get closer to Mom.

After the initial canine onset subsided, I became aware of an enticing scent wafting through the air. Another of Jon's infamous concoctions. This one consisting of roast pork accompanied by roasted fingerling potatoes. I poured a glass of Nobilo Sauvignon Blanc and settled in for a gastronomic experience.

As we dined, I asked Jon if he'd made any progress in his investigation of Flowering Rosemary. Typical of Jon, he had pretty much wrapped the whole thing up in a big red bow.

"Yes, I spoke with several of the vineyard employees and one of the staff from the Culinary Institute. It seems as though they'd hired Ron to get their wine tastings up and running. He was only supposed to be a temporary measure as they learned about the various aspects of the industry. It had always been their intention to find full-time sales staff after their focus on the growing of the grapes and the production of the wine itself had been accomplished."

"So you don't think Ron could have been all that worried about losing income if he'd been exposed?"

"Not only that, they weren't all that well connected within the industry yet, so he wouldn't worry that they could sully his reputation. And they have already moved on, so Flowering Rosemary appears to be a dead end."

"Thanks Jon. That really helps."

"No sweat. Now fill me in on your day."

We discussed my conversation with Tiffany and her revelations about Ron and the boys. Jon nodded his head.

"What?"

"I'd heard some rumors about "trouble in paradise" at Schroeder."

"And you didn't bother to mention them to me?"

"They were just rumors."

So typically Jon.

We spent the rest of the evening playing with the bulldogs and relaxing. We tried to watch an old movie, but the pups had other plans. Luckily, watching bulldogs at play is generally more entertaining than a movie. Once they tired themselves out, we were too tired to care how Joan Crawford was ill-treated by her daughter.

* * *

I was anxious to get into the office to find out if Maxie and Liv had made any progress in their investigation. Greeted at the door by a minor panic on the HR front I was unable to get to either of them before mid-day. I suggested we grab a bite of lunch and share our findings.

The four of us headed out to Mouth of the South in Florence, where we felt safe in discussing issues related to the murder without fear of being overheard – or more importantly, we knew anyone who overheard wouldn't care.

Once we ordered, Cora and I gave the floor to Liv and Maxie. Their story was somewhat more complex than Jon's had been regarding Flowering Rosemary. Cal's suspicions about the books being discrepant in his investment group were not unfounded. Liv had discovered she had a connection to their CPA, Dick Stone, and while he was unable to reveal any details of the account itself, he had been lamenting the fact that his only financial contact was a woman named Joanie.

According to Stone, Joanie was a huge problem. He hadn't been able to determine whether or not she was the dumbest person he'd ever encountered, or she was pretending to be the dumbest person he'd ever encountered. Although Stone was close friends with the major investor in the group, he was on the verge of resigning the business for fear of losing his sanity. She was that bad.

Maxie and Liv had their job cut out for them. They felt the key to the whole business was whether Joanie was making a lot of careless errors, or if she was fully aware of the major discrepancy in the books. If her ignorance was just a ruse, did that mean she was working for someone else, or was she actually the brains behind this plan to siphon money out of the investment account?

Dick concurred that this was indeed the issue, but he lost no time in weighing in that Joanie would have to be an academy award winning actress to actually be intelligent and be able to portray someone that wholeheartedly ignorant.

"So what are your next steps?" asked Cora.

"We need to get to Joanie ourselves and try to determine her level of involvement," Maxie replied.

"But don't you think that could be quite dangerous, all things considered? Don't make the mistake of thinking that because she's a woman she isn't dangerous," Cora countered.

"You make a good point," Maxie responded, "Liv and I just always think we can outsmart anyone. That could be a dangerous assumption."

"True, but we're still going ahead with our plans," Liv added.

"Figures," I replied.

"Try to be particularly careful," Cora cautioned. "Don't just rush in with your usual 'take no prisoners' attitude. Think this one through more carefully, and plan your options."

"Duly noted," Liv agreed.

I wasn't as worried as Cora. Maxie and Liv did tend to believe they were invincible, but they weren't stupid. And they weren't foolhardy. We spent the next half hour discussing my findings from Bartoni, Jon's Flowering Rosemary story and Cora reviewed her revised financial possibilities that were now probabilities. It was an extremely productive lunch hour.

The second half of the day brought no fewer surprises than the morning had. By the time five o'clock rolled around, I had accomplished nothing on my to-do list. It was probably time to pack it in and call it a day. I cleared off my desk and took my empty Diet Sunkist can to the recycling bin. On my way past the oversized worktable near the kitchen doorway, I glanced at an envelope with my name on it. That was odd. I opened the envelope with some degree of trepidation. It was a hand-written note that said:

Dear Donna,

I am, or was, Tim Iremont's girlfriend. We were keeping our relationship secret for reasons that are less important now. After all I've read about you and your murder solving experience, I just knew that you would be helping the police with this investigation.

Donna, I think I might have some information that can help with the case. But I'm reluctant to go to the police and make our whole relationship public. Would you be willing to meet with me so I can share my suspicions with you?

To put you at ease, I would like to meet at the coffeehouse at 114th & Dodge. A public place, but where no one is likely to know me. I'll be there at 9 am tomorrow morning, and I'm hoping you'll join me.

Signed,

Rosie

Holy crap! I could not get home fast enough to share my news with Jon.

Jon surprised me. Twice. First he suggested that meeting with Rosie in a very public place should not prove to be a major health hazard – although he was quick to offer his services hanging out nearby, incognito. I politely declined. And second, he announced:

"I know who did it. I wrote it in a note and placed it in

an old copy of The Gang That Couldn't Shoot Straight."

"Is that a clue?"

"Not necessarily. And even if it was, would that make the investigation considerably easier?"

I had to admit it wouldn't. Mob members were purported to be in and around several of the wine businesses we were debriefing.

The rest of our evening passed uneventfully. I ate my usual diet fare supplemented by mountains of vegetables and Jon had leftovers from the previous evening's feast. Try as I might, I couldn't get my mind off of the meeting with Rosie. It was not the most relaxing of evenings.

I spotted Rosie right away as I walked into the coffee shop. It helped that she was waving furiously and looked to be about the right age for a relationship with Tim. After buying a giant coffee, I joined Rosie at her corner table. She jumped right into her story.

"I haven't admitted this to anyone else, Donna," Rosie started. "I found Tim's body."

"But I heard…"

"Yes, I know. I found it and ran out. I was terrified, both of seeing a dead body and of fear that the killer was still nearby. Once I ran out, I realized I'd probably done something illegal. Believe me, I was prepared to make an anonymous call if he wasn't found quickly, but he was, so I just let it go."

"I can see that you haven't actually let it go."

"True enough. I'll probably never let that vision go. And I'll always be haunted by the knowledge that I left him there. I'm trying to justify my actions by reminding myself that it was too late to help him at that point."

"Rosie, are you sure?"

"Absolutely. I don't believe I would have left if I'd thought there was any hope – there wasn't."

Now I was in an awkward place. This was important information and I knew Rosie expected me to keep her confidence. If Warren knew that I'd held this back, I shudder to think of her reaction. And she'd be right. I was officially an accessory. Shit.

I placated myself by forcing the realization that it really isn't all about me. Maybe I need Clovis around to remind me not to be so self-centered. God forbid!

"So anyway," Rosie recovered faster than I. "When I found Tim's body, I also noticed something that could be a clue."

"You noticed it, and when the police came they didn't?"

Of course I really don't know what the police noticed since they were being so tight-lipped about the investigation. They might have found it. Maybe this would give me some invaluable insights into the case. At this point, I observed that Rosie was blushing deeper and deeper shades of reddish purple. Either she was choking on a scone or something had her seriously embarrassed.

"There may be a reason why the police didn't notice it."

Oh god, I didn't think I was cut out for the life of an

accessory.

"I found that decoration from a key chain lying next to Tim's body. It said NED."

"NED as in three initials, or Ned as in a name?"

"That's just it, I have no idea."

"And you didn't take it?"

"Oh Donna, I would never take a major clue from a murder investigation," Rosie was quick to assure me. "I didn't see it until right before I accidentally kicked it. It shot across the floor and fell into a heating vent. I know better than to tamper with evidence, so I just left it there."

"God Rosie, that could be the single most important clue in this whole thing," I said.

Now Rosie began to tear up.

"You don't have to tell me that. I've been tortured by this whole thing non-stop. I can't sleep, I have no interest in eating. I'm just afraid that if I come forward now, I end up in jail. And I just can't do that, I can't take that chance."

I wish I knew enough to reassure her, but I was thinking she might just be right about that. And knowing what I now know, I could be right behind her in my chic orange jump-suit. This was truly a dilemma – for both of us. It dawned on me that, if we could isolate the owner of the NED trinket, maybe we could find other means of pointing things in his direction. If all else failed, maybe I could ask to see the crime scene and pretend to see something shiny in the grate. My mind was whirling with possibilities when I realized Rosie had been speaking.

"And I did as much research as I felt was safe given my fear of both the murderer and the police."

"Oh, and what were you able to determine?"

"Just that there doesn't seem to be anyone connected with any part of the wine business who is either named NED or who would have a symbol NED. Not unless it means something extremely obscure."

"Nice work, Rosie, that would have been my suggestion." I asked Rosie to brief me on all of her investigative work regarding NED. I wanted to be sure that everything possible was ruled out.

In briefing me, Rosie finally began to relax a bit. She was proud of her work on the case, and I had to admit she'd done a damn fine job of detecting. I even started to see a little bit of a smile peak through. This had to be so incredibly difficult for the poor kid. I even felt a little better about not sharing this tidbit with Warren. Rosie was on top of getting to the bottom of the NED origin. I didn't think the detectives would have handled it any better, I know I certainly wouldn't have. But I was more than a little puzzled. I'd have to do some research on my end.

It seemed like a good time to ask questions about Rosie and Tim and their relationship. More importantly, I was hoping that Rosie could give me some insights on the relationship between Tim and Ed. And she didn't disappoint.

"I can tell you one thing, Tim had an enormous amount of

respect for Ed. He always said Ed taught him everything he knew about the industry."

I kind of wish I'd known that while Ed was still alive. But, even though I couldn't tell him, I was feeling proud of my friend.

"Yes, and Tim made it very clear that others in the industry had a healthy respect for Ed as well. In fact, over the past several years, he had built himself quite a reputation as being the guy who kept the industry honest. Folks were more than a little intimidated by Ed, even some very high-level folks."

"Really, Ed?" Wow, I guess there was a whole lot I didn't know. I just couldn't picture my smart-ass pal as yielding a mighty sword and feared by all. But I was learning.

"Yeah, definitely Ed."

"And Tim said he intimidated experts in the industry?"

"Well, his exact words were more like 'yeah, even some of those big swinging dicks were scared shitless of Ed.' But I thought I'd clean it up just a bit."

Rosie went on to paint a very detailed picture of the almost father/son relationship Tim and Ed had enjoyed. I could tell as she was winding down and reaching the time just before Tim and Ed were murdered, that some of her fears began to push back into her thoughts.

"God, Donna, I've got a huge problem here, haven't I?"

To the extent that I could, I tried to put Rosie at ease. I suggested she consider contacting a lawyer and asking for advice as to whether or not she should contact the police at this point. She hadn't thought of that and was very grateful. I promised to send her the names of some criminal attorneys. She winced when I used the term, but acknowledged that's who would have her answers.

As we parted, Rosie asked two things. She wanted to know what I would do with the lead she'd given me, and she wanted me to keep her informed if the lead proved helpful. I assured her that research on NED was only just beginning, and agreed to keep her in the loop as things progressed. I asked her to keep me informed on how she made out with her attorney and her major dilemma. And she readily agreed.

[CHAPTER 22]

NED. That was going to bug me for some time to come.

I asked everyone what NED could mean besides the name. Nothing. I thought being handed the name of the killer was just too easy. I felt it must be an acronym for something. It was driving me crazy.

After an 11 am meeting, I returned to my desk to see the message light blinking. Jon had left a message that Olivier was concerned about the investigation and wanted us to meet him at the restaurant for a late lunch and a recap.

When we got there, it was evident he was not alone in his concerns. Pascal, Phillippe and Jeannie LaPlage, the Campenellas and Olivier's wife, Desiree, were all in attendance. After I filled them in on the sum total of what I knew and what I suspected, they ran through each lead providing color commentary.

"No," Olivier stated, "Bartoni is a dead end. They don't have the imagination."

Coming from Olivier, that held a lot of weight. As a restaurant and bakery owner, Olivier had not been satisfied that he tapped his full potential. Crime solving had become far more than a hobby for him. In fact, rumor had it that

Olivier was about to make his public service status official. But that was still just a rumor.

"Camerotti should not be overlooked," Phillippe suggested, "regardless of the potential dangers."

"How deeply have Liv and Maxie delved into Cal's investment group?" Pascal offered. "Until you know the background stories of the entire group, as well as their close acquaintances, you will not be able to rule them out."

"When you begin to focus on Camerotti, let us know," offered Phillippe, "we would not want to see you tread on such dangerous ground without our backup and support."

At this point I was feeling a little overwhelmed. There was still so much ground to be covered and so much of it was fraught with untold dangers. This was definitely something new. Even though in my two previous investigations there had been hints of danger, they were nothing like the certain perils of stumbling onto an illegal and high stakes operation that could possibly be mob connected. I looked around at the faces that held hope I would find the answers. Letting them down would be unthinkable, but even with their help I knew I was in way over my head.

I wondered about Warren. She was the lead investigator, and an exceptionally competent detective, but she could also be wandering into dangerous, perhaps even fatal, territory. And yet, she had no choice but to follow the path that the leads took her down – regardless of the consequences. I made a mental note to check on Warren and see if I could detect a level of fear, and if I could perhaps help her work through it.

In retrospect, that could end up being my greatest contribution to this entire investigation. The more I learned about some of these folks, the more I became convinced that arm's length was my best vantage point. I was only relieved that I hadn't made myself a public spectacle to date. It was public knowledge that Ed and I did business together. And so far, in my investigating, I could chalk all of my calls up to either working on the Bohóc brand or planning some sort of social or charity event. Okay, that was a stretch but at least it was something to work with.

It's not like I was particularly proud of my cowardice on this case, but no one would have to warn me to be careful. I was leading with careful.

"Research is clearly the next step," offered Marie Louise, "Dave and I will be happy to burn the midnight oil and compile dossiers on Cal's fellow investors."

Leave it to Marie Louise to help bring things down to earth. Just as I was envisioning my wine drinking comrades in cat suits repelling down the face of a glacier to entrap the bad guys, her comment enabled me to reinvent the visual into a much safer computer in a home office scenario. That was comforting.

"You know," Desiree's comment brought me back from my reverie, "there is a little known database that captures information about most wine-related entrepreneurs, employees and investors. It was begun years ago by a PR firm called NED."

NED??!!?? That was NED? I was speechless and Desiree went on.

"When the wine industry in this country was young, this one particular vintner in upstate New York had delusions of grandeur, and paranoia. He was sure that his secret combination of grapes would be purloined by nefarious and less talented posers and he was determined to keep that from happening. He hired this firm to keep tabs on every new entry into the industry. His strategy was both to know his enemy and to be able to easily destroy his enemy. Over the years, the folks from NED and some of the old wine families have been able to use the database for good rather than evil – but it certainly has the ability to help us dive deep into virtually everyone under suspicion in Ed's murder."

Brilliant! As I sat and listened raptly, Desiree, Dave and Marie Louise made plans to download dossiers on every name we had, and look for more. I texted Maxie to hold off on some of their running around. It was looking as though we'd be saving them a lot of grunt work by using NED.

I decided to work from home for the rest of the day, and maybe in the morning I'd stop by and see how Warren was making out. And maybe I could find out more about some of those junkyard papers. There, I was feeling more like myself already.

The first order of business, after petting and praising

all the bulldogs, was to check in with the office. After being assured of calm waters, I asked to speak with Peg. It had been hours since I'd checked in with my crew and that didn't seem fair. But the first words out of her mouth made me very sorry I had.

"Have you seen it? Clovis's wine blog?" Peg croaked.

Oh god.

"Haven't seen it, can't even imagine it."

Clovis knew nothing about wine. But as a self-declared expert on everything, why should it surprise me that she had deemed herself an expert on wine?

"What is she saying?"

"Well, Donna, Clovis has announced to the world that the wine industry is comprised of a collection of villains and no-accounts who will stop at nothing for the almighty dollar – including murder. She speculates that much of the industry is mob connected."

I rolled my eyes. Peg went on.

"And the best part? She manages to insinuate you in virtually every sleazy aspect."

I fell off my chair. Literally. When I fell, I brought with me my laptop and my ice tea – unsweetened. It hurt. Getting up, I rubbed the spot on my nose that was clipped by a descending laptop. There was nothing I could do about the drenching from a recently refilled ice tea. I guess my foot slipped off the rung.

While picking myself up and wringing everything out,

it dawned on me that my cover had been blown. Regardless of how pointless the drivel meted out in Clovis' blog, the nefarious and "connected" ones would know enough to monitor every online word written about them, and apparently I was highlighted and placed in the middle of it all. I didn't know how Clovis had managed to do it – but she had managed to put my life in danger as well as make a public mockery of me.

"Donna, hey Donna, you alright?"

"Define alright."

"What?"

"Never mind, do go on."

"Do you want the URL?"

"Do I have a choice?"

"Cloviswinereveal.com."

"Fine."

"I'm sorry, Donna."

"Yeah."

After getting off the phone from Peg I spent the next half hour perusing Clovis' blog for any germ of truth or anything that wasn't pure nonsense. No luck. But what did that matter? The public was always anxious and ready for a scandalous revelation – and there was that – in spades. In Clovis' delusional journey through wine country I was the hopeless and hapless amateur sleuth who, determined to put every mob boss in jail, was running frenetically around the countryside gathering flawed proof that these guys had committed every crime from serving a big cab with a light seafood sauce to murdering whole gangs of vintners who got in their way of cashing in on wine-related crimes. In fact, after reading her prose, one would wonder how this news of a current day St. Valentine's massacre could have gone unnoticed by the press. Had I been a card carrying optimist, I might have convinced myself that no thinking person could ever believe any of Clovis' demented storytelling, but I wasn't. I was a Jersey girl, born and bred, and every menacing word I read confirmed my upcoming date with cement shoes and a dip in unholy waters.

I wasn't sure where to turn. The damage had been done and the price would be high. I contemplated calling Clovis to share my grave concerns in an attempt to shut this down. Cooler heads prevailed. Any contact with Clovis now would unleash a string of events certain to lock me in a women's correctional facility where I'd be a sitting duck for mob revenge. I had to keep my head.

I called Liv and Maxie. Liv knew Clovis only too well, and Maxie had the gift of unfailing persuasion. I would set them loose on Clovis.

One hour and twelve minutes later, I got a text from Maxie: It's fine.

Thirty-two minutes after that I received a scathing email from Clovis accusing me of waiting for an opportunity to torture and humiliate her. In fact, I had been waiting for that opportunity and I was now sorry to have missed it.

She went on to say that Liv had "ripped her head off and shoved it down her neck." Clovis claimed to never have been so outraged at the bullying and even violent behavior to which she had been subjected.

From what I was able to piece together from her disjointed ranting, it seems as though Maxie, and Liv in particular, had worked her over royally, while they had Marcy busily editing her blog to highlight which of the information was baseless speculation, to remove the most ludicrous and incendiary of the information and to rewrite my role as a former co-worker who continually warned Clovis of the dangers of sticking her nose into business about which she knew nothing. Apparently, Marcy went on to edit the blog to point out that much of the content was speculation being compiled for a future book of fiction.

By the end of Clovis' email I had laughed myself into a slightly better mood. Clovis' indignation is always funnier from a distance. As much as I appreciated all of their hard work, although I thought for Liv it might have been more personal payback, I knew that at the end of the day the damage had already been done. I did, at least, hold some hope that as the Good Fellas continued to check mentions of themselves online, they would see that Clovis' blog had been outed as the fraud it truly was – and maybe they'd turn a blind eye toward me. Maybe.

[CHAPTER 23]

The next morning dawned early. Everything was in slow motion. Over coffee I decided to take stock of yesterday's fruitful lunch. Step 1, take a good hard look at Camerotti – from a long distance. Oh crap, thinking of Camerotti brought back the whole Clovis blog incident. No wonder things were in slow motion – I may have just moved from minor annoyance to bulls-eye in the minds of the seedier and more dangerous characters in the wine industry. Lingering on this thought would not serve me well. Difficult as it was, I forced myself to continue on my recap of yesterday's lunch.

Step 2, less focus on Bartoni, and step 3, continue to scrutinize Cal's investment group until all involved could be safely ruled out.

So, for now, my focus would be on Camerotti. And that would be the most challenging group to investigate. I would have to call Phillippe to find out what backup and support he had in mind. Being from New Jersey, my thoughts immediately leapt to the possibility that my phone was tapped. Thank you Jersey upbringing for the extra little oomph of paranoia that has served me so well over the years!

I would talk to my confederates at work and make an outline of our approach, then I would contact Phillippe to meet for coffee. We would share nothing incendiary over the phone or through email.

Once showered and dressed, I was almost ready to face the day. I left a few minutes early in order to stop by the station for my "touch-base" with Warren.

As I walked into the station and up to the front desk, I noticed that I was standing next to an extremely dapper gentleman to my left. There was something unmistakably familiar about him, yet I was certain we'd never met in person. At the risk of being rude, I stole a few sideways glances. When our eyes met, I knew I'd been busted. I produced a feeble smile hoping to convey my friendliness to the world and everyone in it.

"Good morning Ms. Leigh. I am Vincenzo Camerotti," he began as he returned the smile. But it was just as feeble as mine and didn't come close to reaching his eyes.

I started to hyperventilate mildly. And yes, within seconds I was greeted by the menopausal menace, the hot flash. As I stood next to him, trying desperately to look nonchalant, I could feel the beads of sweat forming on my temples and my upper lip. The back of my hair became soggy and my armpits drenched. Without moving a muscle, I had transformed from a crisp business woman to a mushy, overcooked hunk of pasta. It's so hard to maintain a tough and fearless demeanor when your traitorous menopausal body has spoken.

I wiped the sweat from my upper lip and responded, "good morning, Mr. Camerotti. I hear great things about your wine."

I know, it was lame, but aside from flop sweat I was pretty much out of tricks; I was dripping profusely, right next to the great man himself.

Mr. Camerotti continued, "what brings you to the precinct on this lovely day, Madam?"

The pause was interminable. I was already at great risk. The thought of the head of the Camerotti family knowing who I was most assuredly did not bode well. Anything I said to this man could up the quotient considerably. If I lied and said something else stupid I could rise higher in the ranks of target, and if I told him the truth, I'd probably be dead before nightfall.

"Pardon me, Sir, but do you find it particularly warm in here?" I asked fanning myself vigorously.

"Please excuse me, madam, I can see that you are in some discomfort. May I help you to a chair?"

"No, thank you, Mr. Camerotti. It will just be a moment and my hot flash will subside, hee, hee, hee."

Now I was a complete blithering idiot. Who says that and then giggles? It's amazing what abject fear will do to a person. After a moment, I felt capable of responding.

"Well, Mr. Camerotti," I began, "I'm not sure if you've heard, but Ed Von Hapsburg of the Bohóc wineries was found dead, and since he was a client of mine, the police have been asking a number of questions in order to rule out foul play."

If he bought that whopper I'd be eligible for an Academy Award. I could feel my sweat glands ramping up even as we stood there.

"Of course, Ms. Leigh, I am very aware of our dear Ed's departure. Such a tragedy. In fact, that is the very reason I stand here myself. But I would have thought that your being here had more to do with your amateur sleuthing. Are you not hot in pursuit of a potential murderer?"

That about did it. Was there nothing sacred? This man must have cameras and bugs all over my home and office. What the hell?

With a bit more righteous indignation than I had any right to display, I replied, "Mr. Camerotti, I am most interested in how you have made all of these assumptions about me."

"Why Ms. Leigh, you are, of course, aware that the entire wine industry in North America is talking about you these days. They all knew and revered our colleague and it is widely known that you have taken on the case. Since word of your crime solving reputation has been making the rounds, you've become something of a legend. I assumed you would know that."

I was shocked. And then, I'm embarrassed to admit, I was pumped. That was the coolest thing anybody had said about me in a long time. It was awesome. Apparently my ego is significantly larger than I had previously imagined. I managed to forget I was standing next to a potentially murderous, probably mob-connected, giant and I was busy jumping up and down because people in the wine industry heard a few rumors about me. That was an important lesson learned – ego trumps fear. Upon hearing Camerotti's voice again, my one-woman celebration came to an abrupt halt.

"So Ms. Leigh, are you indeed here to discuss details of the case with Detective Warren?"

Complete flip back to total paranoia. It was difficult to take it all in. Camerotti not only knew who I was, he knew what I was doing. If he was responsible for Ed's death, that did not bode well for my future.

"Mr. Camerotti, I can assure you that rumors of my crime solving acumen are greatly exaggerated. I can also assure you that, despite rampant rumors, I have never actually solved a murder. I just keep getting the credit."

I told the truth, but I wasn't sure he'd buy it. I figured I'd play really dumb, or ballsy, depending on how you look at it.

"So what brings you to the station, Mr. Camerotti, if I might ask?"

Wow, that was a rush! Challenging a possible mob boss. Oh shit, I just challenged a mob boss!

"I like your style, Ms. Leigh," Camerotti chuckled quietly.

At least I think it was a chuckle, or maybe it was a groan of intent. I didn't know. I just knew that I'd better make my escape before it was too late. At that moment, a young man came out of the back area and addressed Camerotti.

"Sir, Detective Warren asked me to thank you for taking a few minutes to stop in and discuss the case. As the president of the California Wine Co-operative, she is most anxious to get your viewpoint."

Camerotti nodded and I saw my chance.

"Well, I've got to run to a meeting, I'll have to check in with the good detective later. Mr. Camerotti, so nice to have met you, I wasn't aware that you were the Co-op president, blah, blah, blah." And then run!

On my way out the door, I think I heard Camerotti say something polite about meeting me. Investigating his wineries was going to be even more challenging than I had anticipated. Once in the office, I ran to my desk and took some time to catch my breath and calm down. I wondered if Warren would share any of her conversation with Camerotti when I did finally catch up with her. That thought made me chuckle. Even scared witless I couldn't stop thinking about important clues.

I was anxious to get into my ten o'clock meeting. I couldn't think of a better way to put the recent past behind me than to dive right into agency work. Even better, we had a heated battle over a new feature on our website. By the time the meeting ended, Camerotti was nothing but a distant memory. Until I listened to my voicemail.

"Ms. Leigh," the unmistakable voice began. "It dawned on me that you and I might actually be of help to each other. I was thinking it would behoove us to get together for a little light repast this evening. I will be waiting for you at Dante's at 6 o'clock – and I'm never late."

I guessed I'd be having dinner with a mobster that evening. Camerotti didn't leave much room for equivocation. He expected me there and I was not about to disappoint. Unlike my recent coffeehouse meeting, this time I did want back up – and big time. The Jersey in me dictated that I go way overboard, and that seemed like the logical move to me.

I would get Peg and Babs, Phillippe and the rest of the boys from lunch along with Jon. Together we would formulate my discreet, but bulletproof, backup plan. At least I hoped it would be bulletproof.

First I contacted Jon and asked him to round up the guys. Then I grabbed Peg and Babs and outlined our game plan. Within the hour, I had completed a site map for my war games. No stone was left unturned.

Peg and Babs would watch where Camerotti and I sat and they'd get a table in the other section of Dante's. We arranged this with restaurant management ahead of time to ensure a flawless plan. All of the boys would be waiting in Dante's kitchen – since Dave was related to the owners, this was easy for him to arrange.

Peg and Babs would each have a phone with them. One would have 911 waiting at the push of a button and the other would have the boys in the kitchen. Dave would brief the entire wait staff to look for anything untoward and report back to him immediately.

The rest of the day dragged on endlessly. Try as I might, my mind would focus on nothing but my impending meeting with Camerotti. What could he possibly have planned to say to me? Would he threaten me? How would I react to a threat from him? I know I'd never reacted well to threats from angry media sales reps over the years – but this was very different. I never considered sales rep threats to be life threatening. I hoped I'd be able to keep my cool, but in reality, I couldn't keep my hands from shaking.

When I entered the restaurant, Camerotti was already sitting on the bench seat along the back wall. Babs and Peg would sit at one of the high tables placed in the upper section just inside the front door. I hoped they wouldn't be too obvious in their observation of us. We had too much riding on this and Camerotti would certainly be on the lookout for any unusual behavior.

We greeted each other cordially, but formally. Camerotti stood to greet me as was fitting his old-world manners. Once seated, I waited for him to begin – since this was his clambake.

"Thank you for joining me, Ms. Leigh," he began.

"I had the impression our meeting was rather important to you, Mr. Camerotti."

"I don't know if I would call it important. After all, Ed is dead, and nothing any of us can do will ever bring him back. I will personally miss Ed a great deal. As the head of the California co-op, I worked closely with Ed for years and I counted him as a friend."

"Well then, Mr. Camerotti, we have something in common."

"Actually, Ms. Leigh, I believe we may have several things in common."

I felt as though we were in a gym fencing for the advantage. Where was this all going? Before I lost my patience and foolishly leapt in to demand some answers, Camerotti changed the subject.

"I hope you don't mind, Ms. Leigh, I have taken the liberty of ordering our meal. This is a restaurant I always enjoy when I travel to Omaha, and I believe I have created a menu that you will enjoy as much as I."

Old-world manners didn't take into account modern women, but I'd give it to him this time. Besides, good food notwithstanding, I wasn't sure I'd be able to choke anything down sitting here with Camerotti. And I certainly didn't want to drink enough to dull my senses, although I would have to politely accept at least one pour of the wine he had already ordered. At this juncture, I felt Camerotti was ready to get down to business. I tensed in anticipation. At that moment, I heard a loud commotion. I saw objects flying on the other side of the dining room and then, much to my horror, I saw Phillippe, Jon, Dave, Pascal, Olivier and Francois come running out into the dining room. I believe at this point my life flashed before my eyes. The place was a madhouse, and Camerotti calmly observed.

"I believe your friends have suffered a mishap."

"What?" was the best I could do as I seriously started to

hyperventilate.

"Well, something has occurred with your friends at the other side of the dining room that has caused them to signal your friends in the kitchen and instruct them to charge the front and come to your rescue."

I just sat with my mouth hanging open. How could he possibly know?

Sometimes, being inept is the best strategy. Camerotti remained a gentleman and I remained a mute as we watched and waited for the noise to subside. Once things had settled down a bit, it became apparent that Peg had been the one with the phone to the boys in the kitchen. And apparently, Babs had dropped her menu – she'd wanted to hold it in front of her face so that she could peak in our direction unobtrusively. When Babs bent down to pick up her fallen menu, timing was bad. A waiter with a full tray of drinks was just walking by. As they met, the drinks and the table went flying and Peg accidentally hit the call button on her downward journey. Thus, the boys were alerted of the dire emergency and they responded brilliantly.

Apparently, mid-onslaught, one of the guys realized there was no immediate dire threat to my person. Within moments, my cavalcade of rescuers miraculously transformed into a boisterous celebration for some fictitious bocce team or other. I turned to see the revelers cheering and congratulating each other – and then there was champagne. They looped around the other diners and made their way into the back once again, thinking they'd covered their trail. And then Camerotti and I were on our own once again.

I knew my face was beet red as I turned back and smiled sheepishly.

"I guess there's no point in bullshitting now, is there?"

"None."

"A little insurance?"

"Understandable."

That was all that was said. It was enough.

"Ms. Leigh, I'll get right to the point and prolong your agony no further," he offered.

"Oh Mr. Camerotti, I'm not in agony, honestly."

"Figure of speech, although not without merit apparently, knowing as I do of your propensity to throw yourself into murder investigations."

I had that coming.

"I wanted to clarify a few things. First, I come from a family about which much has been speculated. I personally have never been involved in any illegal activities. You don't have to believe me, but I am telling you the truth. I would also like to be forthright in telling you that I am a major investor in Cal Feisty's group. Under the circumstances, I believe that I will be in the position of being suspected on multiple fronts. In order to save you time and me aggravation I will tell you point blank – I had nothing to do with Ed's death. I shared this, and other information, with Detective Warren this morning. It occurred to me that, after seeing you, I would probably gain a place higher up on your suspect list, and I wanted to put a stop to that aspect of your investigation."

Well, that really stung. I mean, am I so obnoxious that it would be torture for him to put up with a few questions?

Yes, I know, I'm an idiot. But I couldn't deny that my nose was out of joint. As a result, I'm pretty sure my righteous indignation shone through like a beacon in a blackout.

"Well, Mr. Camerotti, I can assure you that I will not deem to inconvenience you any further."

"Now, Ms. Leigh, I implore you, do not be offended."

Too late, Bubb!

"I only wish to spare you any further difficulties. Although I may be pure as the driven snow, there are many colorful characters that operate in and around my business and my investments. I cannot be there at all times to insure that you do not meet with an unfortunate encounter – and I wish to avoid that eventuality.

I didn't know whether to feel flattered, or threatened. I did know that getting out of there soon was top on my list. I thanked Camerotti profusely, but reservedly – after all, I was still offended – for the delightful wine and the little food I managed to ingest. And I beat feet out of there.

"In fact, I am well aware that Ed was in the process of investigating Ron for both his duplicity at my winery and his potential theft within my investment group."

"You knew?"

"Ms. Leigh, I am an astute businessman. It is very difficult to conceal anything from me regarding either my business or my investments. And I can assure you there was no reason to have Ed dispatched for the good work he was doing in an effort to protect my interests."

That made a lot of sense. Why kill Ed when he was trying to ensure that Camerotti Vinyards and Camerotti's personal investments were not ripped off. In light of this information, it made absolutely no sense to suspect this man as a potential killer. In fact, I had to question why we were delving into any of the vineyards and the investment group. We already knew that Ron was up to no good, but Ed was on the side of the good guys. I had to remind myself that the inquiries into the wineries had more to do with looking for a potential accomplice of Ron's, one that wanted his or her identity to remain a secret.

It occurred to me that I'd have to view the vintners very differently from here on in. And any questions I might ask them would be in a much different vein. I would be looking to help them rather than have them convicted of murder. And that would make all the difference.

Once outside, I spotted the three vehicles that had transported my posse to the rendezvous site. We all headed back to our house for a stiff drink and a chance to reconnoiter. Phillippe and Francois were positively jubilant. Clearly we needed to get the boys out more, although I had to admit now that we'd escaped to safety, it had been exhilarating.

For the first few minutes, we were busy pouring wine to

a deafening din as they all took turns recounting the debacle from their own unique vantage point.

"We should all feel proud," Francois began.

"Yes, we were pretty badass guys," Olivier concurred.

"Badass maybe, but I feel foolish," Dave interjected.

"Don't look at it that way, Dave. We responded when the alarm was called. How could we know it was a silly mishap and not a true emergency?" Phillippe proclaimed.

They all nodded their heads. Phillippe had ruled. The guys were heroes. And, in fact, I felt they were my heroes. I like to think of myself as being tough as nails, but when push comes to shove, it's so comforting to know you've got the kind of backup I had that night.

Once things calmed down to a dull roar, we began examining the incident for any pearls of wisdom. Perhaps the only noteworthy item was the fact that several of us had witnessed Camerotti's face during his major revelation, and we all felt it seemed genuine. Although none of us were experts in forensic communication, if we thought he was telling the truth, it would be unlikely that his acting skills were so finely honed that he'd fool all of us. Besides, even if he was mob connected, that didn't make him any less a victim of Ron's, and thus a likely supporter of Ed's.

I had to admit to feeling somewhat let down. Earlier in the day I had convinced myself he was the killer, after assessing my knowledge of the facts. For a brief moment there, I felt that Ed's killer was close at hand. In as much as I was relieved that I hadn't been in mortal danger, I was also let down and, if truth be told, feeling stupid. Camerotti's declaration and what appeared to be the facts of all of Ed's investigating meant we were no closer to the truth, and although we could probably rule him out as a suspect, we were not narrowing the field down in any significant way. How could I have been so far off base? That wasn't like me. Or maybe it was.

Time was slipping away from us, and so was Ed and Tim's killer.

[CHAPTER 24]

The fact that I had been looking at things askew really shook me up. Wasting time was one of my pet peeves, but I had to let it go or risk the loss of more precious time.

Willing myself to focus on anything that would feel productive, I finally lit on one salient thought. Pascal had a connection at the police station. I don't know why that hadn't occurred to me before. Perhaps, through him, I could delve into those junkyard papers more deeply. I knew Warren had shared information – or rather the lack of information – but I felt there could be far more to learn.

I phoned Pascal immediately and set him to work on his friend and those papers. That felt better.

Now it was time to determine the next steps. Since Camerotti was involved with both his family vineyard and the investment group, I felt it was time to get both teams together and compare notes, so I set up a lunch meeting to review information.

We dined at Jackson St. Pub. True to its name, a charming recreation of an English pub with stone floors, a beautifully carved wooden bar and old oak pub tables. It was a regular haunt of ours and we held many a management meeting over salads at Jackson St. On those more frustrating days, it was burgers and onion rings.

On this day Cora, Liv, Maxie and I exchanged information on our respective investigations. It appeared as though we'd all gathered a lot of interesting facts, however none of them had yet revealed themselves to be valuable leads in Ed's murder. Man, that was frustrating! We'd all been so vigilant and yet, in many ways, we felt none the wiser.

Maxie and Liv had found a sketchy character or two involved in the investment group, but nothing that set off the mental alarms. There were several of Cal's physician contemporaries, as well as a smattering of wine industry professionals. At first, I found it odd that a vineyard owner would ever want to invest in any other vineyard, but we speculated that true wine aficionados would never be happy to drink only their own wine – no matter how much they love it. And, if you're going to drink it, why not invest and potentially make a little money.

Although they had spoken to several of the investors, with an introduction from Cal, Liv and Maxie did not believe they had uncovered any crucial information. Most of the investors were well-to-do in and of their own right. The wine investment group was a mere amusement and only one of many investments within the personal portfolios of most members. You'd have to be crazy to kill over that.

After we'd reviewed every piece of information in detail, we sat back in disgust. We were not women content with marginal success. We were driven to succeed.

Much to everyone's consternation, Cora suggested we review each piece of information once again. So we did. Painfully and painstakingly. We were nearly through, with no more to show for all of our work, when one little detail seemed to pop out of nowhere. There was a guy in the investment group who didn't fit the profile – at all. His name was Corey St. Ain and he was a winery technician. Unlike the other investors, he had very little money of his own, and there were some runs-ins with the police in his high school days.

By the end of our lunch, we'd all agreed that Maxie and Liv had more work to do. They had to run down St. Ain's current work situation and find out just exactly what kind of criminal record this guy had. We all agreed that, for the short term, checking on Pascal's ability to infiltrate police files and debrief us on the junkyard paperwork would be my main focus.

That afternoon I happily completed all of my backlogged agency work, energized by the knowledge that we might actually be making some real progress on the case.

When I arrived home, Jon patiently awaited the bulldog avalanche before asking about my day. Before I got too far into the shedding of work attire, he suggested we head over to Le Voltaire for an early dinner and a bottle of wine. That sounded so good.

As we entered the restaurant, I saw Nic heading into the

dining room from the kitchen door. Was I getting paranoid, or did his immediate about face have anything to do with the fact that he'd seen me as well? I couldn't imagine that. Nic was one of the friendliest people I knew, and we'd always had a great rapport. Or so I thought. Elana came over and seated us promptly. I shook off the feeling. There had to be something else going on. Having spent time with Clovis, I had become very proficient at recognizing signs of narcissism in myself. Nic was a busy man and I was sure he'd just forgotten something in the kitchen, although I did notice that he never had a chance to greet us that entire evening.

Once seated, we barely had a chance to peruse the menu when we noticed two of our friends, Jules La Plage and Francois Boulevardier, sitting at the bar sharing a light supper. We waved and called them over. Apparently Julius' wife was away on business and Francois' wife was visiting her kids and grandkids back east. As they had just begun, they abandoned their perches at the bar to join us.

Within minutes of their sitting down, Cal and Jane came in with Phillippe and Jeannie close behind. With a few extra tables, all eight of us sat down to a lovely, impromptu dinner party. The wine and the ideas flowed abundantly.

As long as I had him right there, I asked Cal what he knew about the investigation and how it related to his investor group.

"I know that your two pals have been calling our group. Some of the older, crustier cusses have their noses out of joint. They assume they're being accused of everything from fraud to murder."

"Well, Maxie and Liv can be very direct. I'll admit that not everyone responds well to that style. It's kind of a trademark of our industry; shy and retiring women are typically left behind, so we in-your-face types are the ones the world sees."

"Don't get me wrong, Donna, I'm not complaining. You know I like a feisty woman – or I wouldn't have married my Jane here." And he patted her arm affectionately. They were a great couple, Cal and Jane. I tried to press further to see if I could ascertain anything of value from Cal, but he was enjoying his relaxing evening with a good bottle of wine and some great friends. So I let the evening run its own course.

Before dessert was served, Pascal made an entrance. He signaled that he had some information and wanted to discuss it discreetly. I feigned a trip to the ladies' room off the back dining room and met Pascal there.

"My friend, Edgar, the one at the police department, did some checking for me. He said Ed had notes on two of the investors in the investment group. One was a Wall St. broker by the name of Clive Dorsey. He said Dorsey had suffered some losses in his clients' portfolios and he had started to lose some of his bigger clients. His own investments weren't doing all that well, so he seemed like a person to watch. But there was really nothing more than that. The other guy was Corey St. Ain. That got my ears perked up. His greatest concern about St. Ain was that he really didn't fit the investor profile, mostly in that he had virtually no money to invest. In fact, it appeared as though St. Ain had invested every penny he had in this group. Everything, that is, except for about 15 grand that he kept safely in his local bank – until a few weeks ago, that is. According to Ed's files, St. Ain was employed by Camerotti, and he followed the great man around like a little puppy, almost to the point of being unstable.

Wow, that was the motherlode, and suddenly my radar was pointed directly at St. Ain. I mean, there were other areas that still required some checking – but a whole lot of questions began popping into my mind about St. Ain: his working for Camerotti, his being in Cal's investor group, his not fitting the profile of an investor, his sinking all of his money except for 15 grand into the group – and then taking his last remaining 15 grand out of the bank. That was a lot of 'unusual' for one guy. I rejoined our group and brought Pascal with me. We all enjoyed a round of Calvados before calling it a night.

[CHAPTER 25]

The next morning my entire focus was on St. Ain. Probably the best place to start would be in establishing an alibi. I needed to know where he was on the days surrounding Ed's demise. Had he been in Omaha or back in his California office? I wanted to glean this information without tipping my hand. If St. Ain was who and what I thought, he would be extremely dangerous.

I waited until it was 9 am in California and put a call through to the Camerotti front office. I introduced myself as a representative of his credit card company and explained that I wanted to verify his whereabouts during the week of Ed's murder, explaining that there had been some unusual activity on the card. Sweat formed on my brow and upper lip as I awaited the receptionist's response. I was aware that I could be looking at some federal jail time if I got caught perpetrating this fraud.

"Let me get him for you," the jewel-toned receptionist voice offered.

"Oh no, that won't be necessary," I scrambled for a credible reply, "No need to bother him, this is just a cursory, routine check. Can you just tell me if he was in the office that week?"

After a brief pause, Ms. jewel-tone replied, "well, I suppose there's no harm in telling you that Mr. St. Ain was attending to business as usual that whole week."

And with that one remark, she punctured a massive hole in my brilliant solution to the case. It couldn't possibly have been St. Ain; he was nowhere near Omaha. The realization that my brilliant solution was a bust took more of a toll than I'd expected. I was so sure. Now I'd have to start all over again, and there was no other suspect that fit the facts anywhere near as perfectly.

Well, as the great Sherlock Holmes always said "when you have eliminated the impossible, whatever remains, however improbable, must be the truth." St. Ain was the impossible, and must therefore be eliminated. Little did I realize then, Liv and Maxie would not be quite so quick to acquit St. Ain.

I sludged my way through the morning to-do list with a sour attitude and pessimistic outlook. By noon I realized I needed an attitude adjustment if I was to be any good to myself or the investigation. I checked with Cora and she felt that we might want to give a bit more attention to the murder of Ed's distribution manager, Tim. That made sense, we had really glossed over that murder since Ed's was the one that had hit closest to home. Perhaps there was more to learn from the second murder. Hell, we hadn't even visited the scene of the crime.

That perked me up quite a bit. It was time for another road trip. Cora rounded up Peg and Babs, and we were off to another precarious leg of our adventure. And then lunch.

* * *

We arrived at the distribution center and parked Peg's giant SUV out by the loading dock. None of the yellow crime scene tape remained, so we wouldn't be breaking any laws – initially.

We made a thorough sweep of the outside before venturing in. It appeared to be fairly deserted, not surprising all things considered. We were just trying to get a lay of the land so we'd be able to recognize any potentially useful information. It was fairly evident that the most recent activity had been a virtual fleet of municipal first responder vehicles, not at all the normal beverage trucks picking up product. Once we confirmed the obvious, it was time to head inside.

Upon entering we began to look for employees, but there were none in sight. Someone had to be here or the doors would not be unlocked. For fear of unwanted accusations of entering unlawfully, we continued our search. After about 10 minutes, a young woman entered the building through the rear.

She didn't seem at all nonplussed by our appearance, but she did strike me as being world weary.

"Hi, I'm Kayla," she introduced herself, "I'm the assistant distribution manager, how can I help you?"

We expressed our condolences for her loss, and then explained that we were friends and former colleagues of Ed's trying to help the police with the investigation. Kayla offered to give us a full tour of the facilities, so we started in the front office and worked our way back into the warehouse.

Just inside the door to the warehouse we saw the tape outline of Tim's body. That was sobering. It was clearly no less disturbing to Kayla.

"No matter how many times I see it..."

"This must be incredibly difficult for you, Kayla," Peg offered. "Losing Tim must be devastating."

"You have no idea."

We did our best to try to distract her from this grisly reminder of her loss by asking a million questions, some were genuine and some feeble attempts at misdirection. We were groping.

"This warehouse seems really full, are sales slow?"

"You don't have much extra room in this warehouse, will these shelves be emptied out soon?"

"How often do trucks come to make pickups?"

As we worked our way through this process, I couldn't help but wonder why the murderer had returned to kill Tim after the papers had been stolen, so I took a shot:

"Kayla, we've heard rumblings that the killer found a key among the papers. In that theory, he came back to locate whatever that key had secured, and Tim caught him in the act. Does that seem at all plausible based on what you know?"

Kayla knew nothing about a key, but she acknowledged

that she had been struggling with the same puzzling issue, and our theory would explain why things happened as they had. She also acknowledged that having a key to the most important information, haphazardly placed in a pile of less important information would have been consistent with Ed's personal approach to security.

We continued with our grueling process. Poor Kayla was such a good sport. We were rapid fire and relentless. As she deftly fielded our questions, she also attempted to give us a sense of how the warehouse was broken up into varietals, and how the logistics of fulfilling each order worked.

Back and forth, up and down, seemingly endless lanes filled with bottles of Ed's specialty Hungarian wine. He had amassed one hell of an operation. This was quite impressive. We'd seen the warehouse before as his ad agency, but fully stocked was a different experience altogether.

Kayla explained to us that this was one of the few times when the warehouse was filled to capacity, and with the police investigation and the company's loss of two of their most senior people, things had slowed to a crawl. She did explain, however, that trucks were scheduled to begin clearing things out over the next few weeks.

Kayla also expressed concern that some of the buyers were balking at paying the full negotiated price. They were taking advantage of the company's tragedy and there was little she could do to prevent it. She even went so far as to comment that they'd have been better off had Tim's killer set the warehouse on fire on his way out. That was quite shocking to hear.

"Look guys, I'm sorry to subject you to my whining," she apologized.

"Think nothing of it," I reassured her, "you've been through so much, what with losing Tim and having to come to the scene of his murder every day, and you really don't have anyone to listen to your concerns, all alone out here."

As Kayla and I discussed her situation and commiserated, Peg and Babs were drawn to the far corner of the warehouse. In retrospect, it should have struck a nerve.

"Kayla?" Babs interrupted, "it looks like something is stuck under the shelving of this varietal, but I think I can..."

"Oh Babs, be very careful with that particular shelving unit..."

Kayla barely got the last comment out of her mouth as she raced over to the corner where Babs had found a way to shift the weight of the shelving unit and free the random piece of paper. And then we heard a rumble. Simultaneously, there was a mighty roar from Kayla, followed by a mightier roar from the shelving unit as it pitched forward shooting shelves of newly bottled Hungarian wine into the stratosphere, or at least into the warehouse ceiling.

It was more impressive than the coolest light show. Glass shattered and wine and glass sprayed everywhere. Although it probably took no more than five minutes, it seemed much longer. As bottles followed their trajectory throughout the four corners of the warehouse, they randomly selected other innocent bottle victims tucked away on shelves throughout the facility. On occasion, the impact managed to unleash an entire shelf, starting a domino effect of its own. As we watched in awe, ducking occasionally as the worst of the bottle shards whizzed by, it was nothing short of a miracle that none of us suffered a severed artery – the five of us became increasingly wine-drenched. From the tip of our heads to the toe of our shoes, we turned a rich, deep purple.

Once the last bottle had shattered and the last ounce of wine had settled onto the concrete floor, all was silent. And then there was laughter. Cora, Peg, Babs and I stood and watched Kayla begin to get hysterical. Just as Peg was about to suggest an ambulance, Kayla managed to get her hysteria under control.

"Oh god, Kayla, I'm so sorry."

"Forget it, Babs, I think you really did us a favor. The insurance money will probably net us more than these vultures trying to take advantage of our troubles, and it will be a lot easier than worrying about the logistics of selling the wine. And the beauty of it all is that I have four impeccable witnesses to swear I had nothing whatsoever to do with this epic mishap. Ironically, Babs, the smashed wine was the stuff we were going to have to let go for well under market value, so you've done us a real favor."

I shot Babs a "you will not play the hero role" warning look to quell the beginning of puffed up pride that I could see emerging on her entire countenance. She checked herself tout de suite and adopted a more appropriate look of humility.

"Anyway, Donna, what about this paper?" Babs managed to ask while holding up a sopping wet square.

I looked it over and was at a loss. While it looked vaguely familiar, I really couldn't make it out. It was a small piece of note paper with a distinctive insignia, one that I was sure I'd seen before, but just couldn't place. There was also a truncated and cryptic note on the paper, and I could swear I'd seen that handwriting before, but for the life of me I just couldn't place either one at the moment. The wine dripping from both the paper and Babs didn't help my attempts at recognition. I would need to think, and shower – a very long, hot shower.

I needed a shower, but that was not yet to be. We began to make our goodbyes and excuses to Kayla, when she pointed out a blinding flash of the obvious.

"Your car will be ruined if you all get in like that."

Damn. But even in crisis, Kayla was quick with solutions.

"I have some warehouse coveralls in the locker room. You need to change and bag your clothing before you head out."

We followed Kayla like obedient little puppies as she led us to the locker room with wine colored towels – very smart – and matching wine colored coveralls. I felt it was less of a brand statement and more of a pragmatic touch. Let's face it, any accident in this facility was bound to turn everything it touched to a burgundy shade, much like us.

Grateful for her wisdom in the face of crisis we thanked Kayla, grabbed the plastic bag full of dripping clothing, and made our way out of the crime/accident scene. Naturally, the fact that any remaining evidence had been compromised beyond recognition hastened our departure. Even the one scrap of paper that was a potential clue was a soggy mess and difficult, if not impossible, to read anymore.

No triumphant lunch for us today. We picked up our vehicles and headed to our respective homes in an attempt to make ourselves presentable for the rest of the day. In an interesting side note, it took about a week for us to wash the tinting effects of what can only be described as a wine car wash from our skin and hair. Yes, we were forced to maintain a low public profile or risk a public reaction much like that of the Blue Man Group. Even Cora, with her gorgeous mocha glow was sporting a rosier demeanor for the next several days.

I'm sure scientists would refute my claim, but I could swear there was a low grade accompanying buzz throughout that week as well. In any case, I had one of the more relaxed and laid back weeks than I'd had in a long time – perception vs. reality – who gives a cork.

[CHAPTER 26]

Although feeling slightly buzzed, the next day my thought process had been somewhat restored. I set to work, examining our precious – and now dry – clue.

Once again, I racked my brain trying to place that insignia. As I thought back through years of stored memory, I began to get that glimmer of recognition. I was pretty sure it was a fairly recent memory, within the past 3 or 4 years, and I was pretty sure there was some connection to wine. And then it hit me. It was a local sommelier group. Members could be found in most of the high end restaurants around the city. But the handwriting. This had to be written by someone I knew well enough to recognize the writing. That narrowed down the field quite a bit. I was closest to the staff at Le Voltaire. As soon as that thought occurred to me, I dismissed it. After all, I knew all these people. They were friends. I knew none of them could be involved in Tim's murder, much less Ed's. That was just not possible.

I decided to focus on the message. Some of the words were missing, and some were blurred. The best I was able to make out was:

"*there at 8 tonight.* And then something like: *Not a big*

deal, I'm sure we'll get it worked out."

Was this the note from the killer to Tim, the one that invited Tim to his ultimate demise? I felt a chill.

It occurred to me that Detective Warren would want to see this ASAP. Since it seemed as though the whole city knew about our little wine mishap – what were they calling it on Facebook? – "Stomping the grapes – Smashing success!" The photos were particularly unflattering. They all needed to get a life. At any rate, I knew Warren would be up to speed on our little misadventure, so she would know precisely when this piece of evidence came into my possession.

I placed a call to the station and left her a message. Then I joined a work meeting in progress. They stopped just long enough to compliment me on my wine-shaded skin and hair and to remind each other that my brain was most likely experiencing a similar effect. I was starting to think we'd all be better off if I just went home and showered until the last vestige of grape was down the drain.

After the meeting I had a return message from Warren. She would swing by the agency and pick up my purported clue. Hmmph. I wasn't sure what she meant by that. Didn't she believe me? I guess I offended her by suggesting that the homicide detectives had missed a crucial piece of evidence left at the scene. In retrospect, I probably should have thought that through and phrased it a tad differently. Oh well, it was all water under the bridge at this point.

Warren was there within 20 minutes. I grabbed the

nearest empty conference room and we sat down to go over my lead. I started by trying to mend my fences.

"Hey listen, Detective, I didn't mean to imply..."

"No worries, Donna, I realize my message might have been somewhat clipped. Trust me, I'm not that sensitive, just having a tough day. The Mayor is on the Chief's back about wrapping this one up, and we're not as close as I'd like to be. You know how it goes."

Holy cow! That sounded like every homicide detective in every cheap murder mystery I'd ever seen. I felt just like the cheap gumshoe.

"Roger that, Detective, the heat is on."

"Roger that? I guess what I heard about the grape seeping into your brain was true. Based on your new look, I'd say everything was compromised."

Once again I had gone too far, and there was a price. But why was it always me feeling like a moron? I imagined that my elderberry complexion was deepening to a near blackberry hue and my addled brain worked itself through the maddening stages of humiliation. Warren kindly sat in silence until I felt my face was no longer a blast furnace. Although I do believe I caught a snicker or two, we were able to resume our conversation shortly.

"Now that I'm here, am I ever going to see this 'lynch pin to the entire investigation?"

Now that Warren was quoting me, I began to see that I may have been a tad over-zealous in my description of the paper we found at the scene.

After another moment of shade deepening thought, I was ready to hand over the holy grail of overstatement. As I handed the piece of paper to Warren, I could see her wheels turning. After a moment to thoroughly examine the evidence she began:

"You familiar with the group?"

I nodded.

"Barely."

"Handwriting?"

"I think so."

"But you can't place it exactly?"

"Right."

"I'll take it back and have the lab boys take a look at it. Maybe they can come up with a fingerprint through all the wine stains." I winced. "And you'll call me when you recall the identity of the writer?" I nodded again. "In the meantime, we'll visit some of the chef-owned restaurants around town looking for a handwriting match."

I guess there wasn't much to say.

"One more thing, Donna. If you recognize the handwriting, isn't it most likely that it's someone from Le Voltaire?"

"No, it's not anyone there."

"You're certain?"

"Absolutely!"

I could see the doubt in her eyes. I wondered if the doubt in mine was as obvious.

"Shouldn't you be looking at Ron first, since he's been the crux of all of this insanity?"

"You know his handwriting?"

"No."

"That's what I thought. Look, don't take it so hard, we'll check him out, but you have to admit it makes the most sense to start with the folks you know best, right? You know, merely as a formality."

Formality my ass. I did have to agree. But I didn't have to like it.

* * *

Back home that night, I replayed my conversation with Warren for Jon's reaction. As I recanted the brief and embarrassing encounter, I also showed Jon a photocopy I'd made of the clue.

"First of all," he began, "It's unlikely that Warren bought your vehement claim of innocence on behalf of the entire Le Voltaire staff."

I had to acknowledge the veracity of that statement.

"And second, I recognize the handwriting too, but I think the individual made an attempt to disguise their actual penmanship. That's making it much more difficult to recall.

I knew instantly that Jon was right. It was a hand with which we were both familiar. Had I just inadvertently signaled the police that the murderer was someone at Le Voltaire?

Now I was on another mission. I needed to pinpoint the handwriting before the homicide detectives did. I figured I owed it to all of the innocent folks not to drag them through a potentially embarrassing process – and potentially damaging to the staff and the restaurant if word got out. I was still sure no one on that staff could murder anyone – but I was left with no choice but to do the legwork.

"Hey Jon."

"Let me guess, you want to have dinner at Le Voltaire tonight?"

I hate it when he reads my mind.

When we stepped into the bustling restaurant, we were immediately struck by the likelihood that there would not be an available table. And we were right. Although we normally preferred the cozy ambiance of a table for two, tonight was different. We'd have maximum potential for exposure to the staff seated at the bar – and thanks to our late arrival – we wouldn't draw any undo suspicion by doing so. We squeezed into the two remaining seats and greeted four or five of the wait staff before ordering our bottle of wine. This just might work.

Jon and I had searched for a means of getting as many of the staff to share their handwriting as possible. Over the course of the next few hours, we shared the kind of lame fact that we were stuck on a word puzzle – a kind of anagram. We feigned frustration and pretended to have turned it into a contest to see who would emerge victorious. The staff, always so eager to enhance a guest's evening, jumped in with both feet. Within a short time, it became clear that the women were on my side, and the men on Jon's.

One by one, we managed to get each staff member, including the kitchen staff, to write something. I was kind of glad that Olivier was not present on this particular evening because, although he had trained his staff to please guests, he might frown on the game Jon and I imposed on his busy staff. But god bless them, they were troopers. They managed to keep our game going without missing a beat in serving their remaining customers.

I couldn't help but notice one oddity. Each time we enlisted Nic to help with the game, his hands were full of glasses and wine or dishes of scrumptious food in need of delivery. He would nod and acknowledge us, but never managed to pick up a pen. Was he avoiding it, or was I being paranoid? In retrospect, I rarely ever saw him empty handed. Even in social settings, Nic was so helpful in ensuring that everyone had a full glass and a timely food delivery.

I realized I was just being unrealistic, and besides, I was certain the handwriting was not Nic's. Although, he was the official sommelier of the restaurant, that notepad could have been accessed by virtually any of the staff, and come to think of it, probably by many of the patrons. I did still have the odd feeling that Nic was not quite himself. And then it dawned on me, Nic had been especially close to Olivier and Ed. Of course Nic would be acting strangely, he was a sensitive guy and he cared deeply about his friends. Losing Ed had to be unbearable for him. I couldn't believe that hadn't occurred to me before.

By the end of the evening we were fairly certainly who had not written the note, and none the wiser as to who had. That was disappointing. I had hoped to find the culprit to keep Warren and her team from barging in and upsetting Olivier's business. But that was apparently not to be.

It was time to turn my attention to another aspect of the case; I had expended enough energy on this note, and to no avail.

[CHAPTER 27]

The next morning I made a beeline for Liv and Maxie. We made arrangements for them to bring me up to speed on their side of the investigation over a quick lunch later that day.

I grabbed Cora, filled her in on all the latest and then set about to complete an article I'd been procrastinating about long enough. As I sifted through the article, I realized it was nearly complete, so I sent it off to proofing and resolved to dive into another project.

Before long, the phone rang and it was Eva.

"Listen Donna, I can't tell you how much I appreciate your attempts to solve these mysteries. I mean no one wants to get to the bottom of this whole mess more than I, but I'm calling to beseech you to let it be. I say that out of love, Donna. You and Jon have always meant so much to Ed, and I can't bear the thought of something happening to endanger your life. As I keep saying, the only thing we know for sure is that we're dealing with someone extremely dangerous. I've already lost Ed and my good friend, Tim. Please don't place yourself in the line of fire over this."

This caught me very much by surprise. I had never known Eva to be so emotive, and I was more than a little surprised that she seemed undaunted by the fact that Ed's murder was far from being solved. Her call was so unexpected I couldn't help but reflect once again on whether the old tenet about the spouse usually being to blame wasn't true in this case as well. But I quickly shook off all thoughts that Eva could ever be involved in anything so horrific.

Based on the intensity of her request, I felt it best to assure Eva again that I would immediately stop all investigating and return my focus to advertising and advertising alone. Although she thanked me profusely, I couldn't help but detect a note of skepticism in Eva's voice when she hung up. Was it possible that even though she had nothing to do with the murder, Eva had reasons for not wanting the killer to be brought to justice? I couldn't help but feel her impassioned plea was over more than her concerns for my safety.

My naturally suspicious mind – remember I do hail from New Jersey – took me in several bizarre directions before I was able to convince myself she was, in fact, just concerned for my well-being. At first, I wondered if she knew the killer and wanted to protect him or her. Was it possible she had a lover who was the killer? Or perhaps a family member? Then, I considered the possibility that if the truth came out, the insurance payout would be diminished. I resolved to spend a few minutes researching insurance claim scenarios before heading out to lunch with Maxie and Liv.

As one might expect, the first few minutes of our lunch were spent in relaying my conversation with Eva, and discussing the possibilities.

"I think it's entirely possible that Eva is just freaked out at the thought of losing someone else close to her," Maxie pontificated.

"Yes, and she has to be feeling completely out of control with her husband and friend brutally murdered. Keeping you safe would most likely help her to regain her sense of control and provide her with some comfort," Liv added.

That did make sense. When you looked at it through the eyes of these wise women, it was not nearly as sinister as I'd begun to believe.

"When you put it that way," I acknowledged, "that all makes sense."

"Yes, and from everything we know about Eva, she was totally devoted to her husband and daughter." Liv closed the lid on that pot so we could move on to the next subject.

Maxie began to excitedly share a scenario involving St. Ain. She and Liv had done their best to map out his movements for the eight weeks prior to Ed's murder. They had done a remarkable job of using social media and a few lame phone calls, combined with debriefing several of Cal's co-investors, to create an extremely detailed overview of St. Ain's every move during that time period.

While there were still a number of unanswered questions, their account painted a surprisingly credible profile of a guy who got carried away, invested in over his head, clashed with Ron unsuccessfully on a number of fronts and had reason to fear Ed's investigation a great deal. As they filled in each question mark, the story grew tighter. And then they came to the end.

"But St. Ain was nowhere near Omaha when Ed's car was tampered with," Liv concluded.

"Yeah, that's the one major piece of the puzzle we can't make fit," Maxie concurred. "St. Ain was at a wine tasting in Napa the night before Ed was murdered, and he was visiting another Napa vineyard on the actual day of the murder. We just can't get around that."

"So you're saying St. Ain had an accomplice?" I asked.

"No, we think that's probably too farfetched, too cloak and dagger to be real," Liv reasoned.

"Yeah, that level of planning and precision seems un-likely when you realize St. Ain is just a cling-on of the rich and famous. He's no great intellect. We see him as committing a murder opportunistically, not as diabolically as this would imply," Maxie explained.

"Well, if you recall..."

"Yes Donna, we know you ruled out St. Ain already, but we just can't shake this feeling we both have that he's involved up to his carafe!"

"I have to admit, I have a great deal of respect for instinct. And you two are almost as intuitive as I am."

A double eye-roll. You didn't see that very often.

"So where are you directing your efforts now? On that other investor, what's-his-name?"

"Yeah, we'll turn a part of our attention to Clive Dorsey," Liv agreed, "he's next on our list."

"But we're not done with Mr. St. Ain quite yet, despite all indications that his hands are clean. Something about him screams out-of-control and desperate. There's no better combination for murder than that," Maxie observed.

For the rest of lunch, Maxie and Liv proceeded to share their process for running down Dorsey. Since he was a local, they expected to be able to get even closer to his activities. I was quick to caution them that, since he was a local, the danger level to them would also rise exponentially, and I was glad I had. I could see from their glance at each other, neither had considered themselves to be in any danger. That would leave them extremely vulnerable in investigating a local crook with excessive resources at his command. Not saying that Dorsey was a crook as much as an unfortunate investor, but at times like these, the distinction could cost them their lives.

After exacting promises from both of my cohorts to be a shade more conscientious about their personal safety, we all headed back to the office where we were prepping for a major new business presentation. There was a lot of work to be done.

By mid-afternoon I was up to my eyeballs in the logistics of my presentation. Things were moving along far more smoothly than I would have imagined (i.e. no writer's block). The hardest thing is to write on command. I don't know how our copywriters do it, but the fact remains, for most of us, the minute we're expected to write on a timeline – we freeze up. That makes these presentations so much more painful. The total absorption in my presentation is what I blame for what happened next.

The phone rang. I answered it without looking.

"DONNA!"

I heard the familiar shriek/whine. Oh god, Clovis. I knew that with the one simple gesture of answering the phone, I had screwed up the rest of my day – and possibly my week. I had forgotten how purely blissful life could be when there was an absence of Clovis. What had I done?

"There you are!" she barked.

And just where did she think I would be?

"I cannot believe you have gone this long without so much as checking in to see how my investigation is progressing. I thought you cared about Ed, but clearly I was wrong."

"And how is your investigation going, Clovis?"

"Oh sure, NOW you want information."

"You called me, remember?"

"Don't get smart with me, Missy. I have been working my fingers to the bone to get to the bottom of this horrific crime, and from everything I hear, you are making the wine circuit into a wine circus!"

I had to give her that one.

"I knew if I took my eyes off you for one minute…."

"Yes Clovis, we all know I'm nothing without you. Now,

did you have a point?"

"Don't try and rush an artiste, Donna."

I wonder if she felt the roll of my eyes.

"Let me just start with those critical and missing papers."

"Actually, Clovis, I found out that there really wasn't much worth learning from the papers that the police reviewed."

"Well, maybe that's because they didn't review the really important papers, as I have managed to do."

Now she had my attention.

"As you know, the police only managed to capture a portion of what Ed had in his investigation. I knew from my wine industry insiders that he had a whole slew of information on the odd behaviors of Clive Dorsey, yet I heard nothing about Dorsey papers held by the police. I decided to conduct my own little investigation, because I am in firm belief that Dorsey holds the key to this whole mystery. He was in serious financial trouble and in a flat out panic. I know this from a conversation I had with him at a recent wine event in Napa."

"Wait a minute. Dorsey told you he was in serious financial trouble?" Now I was beginning to really regret having picked up the phone. Once again, she lulled me into thinking that she had something of relevance to impart, and now...

"Of course not, Donna. Don't be daft! I hear plenty of rumors from my other inside contacts and I could see that Clive was a nervous wreck and covered in flop sweat for the better part of the evening. That's when I realized that the rumors I'd heard were undoubtedly true."

"Well, that's not absolute confirmation, but it would make sense."

"Oh be still my heart! I have the great Donna Leigh's approval. As if I ever wanted it."

She could be a sarcastic little snot.

"What do you want, Clovis?"

"I want to tell you that I had to get my hands on those papers. So I paid several of those homeless men who hang around the dump to keep their eyes open for a box of papers. Apparently, one of them had already confiscated a full box of Ed's papers before you or the police ever got to the dump in the first place. With the money I offered as incentive, he was happy to trot off and grab his treasure to turn over to me. So now I am in possession of some of the most damning papers that have ever existed relating to a wine investor."

I was stunned. I had forgotten that with all that self-involved nonsense, Clovis really did have some impressive gray matter. Let's face it – it rarely showed itself. Her life was far more about working non-stop to ensure her place at the center of attention to bother about thinking. This was one of those rare occasions.

"Clovis, I always believe in giving credit where credit is due. That was inspiring!"

"Yes, I know. But now I find myself on the horns of a dilemma."

And now we knew she wasn't all that gracious in the

face of a genuine compliment. Big surprise.

"How so?"

"Well, naturally, I've read through all the papers and I am mentioned in a somewhat compromising light."

"Really?" I was thankful this was a phone call as I struggled to suppress a smile. I only hoped she couldn't detect it in my voice.

"Yes Donna. Dorsey and I had discussed some of his investments. He had offered to let me in on a few of his choice finds, you know, because he thinks I'm really attractive and wants to get to know me better."

"So you fell for a line and invested in a bogus deal?" I try to cut right to the chase. And now the laughter was threatening to bubble up to the surface. I was hoping I could cut this call short.

"I don't know why you think it was a line! I'll have you know that men everywhere are drawn to my many assets. It's a known fact."

It was like Christmas morning. I knew eventually there would be an upside to this whole hideous situation. And here it was.

"So what are you worried about, Clovis?"

"Oh Donna, I'm just afraid I may have inadvertently tapped into something illegal. I could go to jail, or worse, I could be the killer's next victim."

"As much as I'd love to get a look at those papers myself, I suggest you head right on over to Warren and turn them in, along with yourself."

"I can't."

"Why not?"

"I may have run into Warren shortly after retrieving the papers, and she may have asked if I had anything noteworthy in my possession. How was I to know that these papers would implicate me, Donna?"

"So you lied to Warren?"

"I did."

"While that's not ideal, I do think she would understand and appreciate..."

"It's out of the question. That's why I came to you. You have to help me scour these papers for something that will get me off the hook."

It was with great delight that I informed her Maxie and Liv were conducting the investigation on Dorsey and they would be delighted to work with her in uncovering a way of getting her butt cleared. Clovis jumped on the prospect of having two fine minds working for her salvation.

"And Clovis, I think your concern about being the next murder victim might be a little premature. What makes you think that anyway?"

"My instinct tells me the killer knows I have the papers. And you know that I hail from a long line of Romanian gypsies. We know things."

I could no longer dispute her claim. As annoying as she was, Clovis did know things. If she thought the killer was targeting her, he/she probably was.

I knew it wasn't funny, but I couldn't suppress an onslaught of the giggles much longer. The thought of Liv and Maxie dying to get their hands on those papers, but having to appease Clovis in order to get them, the fact that Clovis was squirming about her illegal doings and fearful of the killer, just cracked me up. What can I say, in Jersey – we're all about the dark humor.

[CHAPTER 28]

I waited a bit before checking in on Liv and Maxie. Liv was fit to be tied.

"You know, Donna, I knew you had a warped sense of humor, but I guess I never realized you're just downright mean!"

That was it. The giggling started all over again. Maxie just shook her head. She hadn't had the pleasure of working with Clovis, so she was in for a real treat.

I tried three different times before the laughter subsided enough for me to review my phone call with Clovis. Even then there were parts of the conversation that started things up all over again. It had been awhile since I'd had such a good belly laugh. I could feel the abdominal muscles tighten up as I spoke.

"You are enjoying this just too damn much," Liv snorted.

"I know, I'm sorry," was all I could get out before cracking up all over again. "I just want to be sure that you understand what's really going on so you don't waste any more time on Clovis than absolutely necessary."

Apparently that last comment gave Liv the wherewithal to put up with my excessive enjoyment of the situation. She allowed me to finish my comments. Once finished, Maxie and Liv invited me to join them for an after-work drink with Clovis. I left, shaking my head no and trying to control one last burst of laughter. I could see from Liv's face it wasn't appreciated.

* * *

At home that night, I played with the bulldogs while recanting the events of the day to Jon. He listened patiently before making his ultimate pronouncement.

"Dorsey is a dead end."

"What makes you say that?"

"The stuff Ed collected was all the information fed to him by the rest of the investor group. Dorsey knew the jig was almost up. While Ed had some very damning information on paper, those were not the only copies and Ed was not the only one who knew everything. The group brought Ed in to tie things up in a neat little package and deliver it to the police so no trail could be traced back to them, but Dorsey knew full well they were onto him, so if he killed Ed, he would have to kill at least a dozen others, and probably not Tim."

"How do you know all this?"

"I listen."

That was a low blow.

"Look, I'm not saying the police shouldn't run down the information on Dorsey. They have to follow every lead just to be safe, but the facts speak for themselves. Killing Ed would not be all that much help to Dorsey."

I thought through everything I knew to date. Dave and Mary Louise had gathered an impressive array of detailed information. I had to admit, based on their findings, Jon's logic was unassailable. That was annoying enough without the crack about listening. This was not shaping up to be my night.

A little more playtime with the bulldogs put me in a much better frame of mind. By eliminating Dorsey, I felt that all the focus must then be placed on St. Ain. But how? I liked St. Ain for the crime because even though he was the one individual firmly ensconced in Camerotti, as well as the investment group, he remained a bit of an outsider in both. It didn't appear as though there was a wide circle of people following anything he did. And isn't that what they say about some of the most famous of crooks – they are so vanilla they can always sneak by unnoticed. Yes, that had to be the key to this whole thing, St. Ain had found a way to sneak by unnoticed – and that's how he managed to kill Ed.

With the strength of my new resolve, I resolved to turn up the heat on St. Ain.

* * *

I arrived at the office in a flurry of activity. I was determined to gain some insights on St. Ain. Perhaps I could run some holes through his alibi. It seemed my best shot, without hopping on a plane for Napa, was to debrief Cal on any remaining details he could recall about St. Ain. First, I re-read the notes from Dave and Mary Louise, and then I called and asked Cal to meet me for coffee later that morning. After that, I filled Cora in on my thoughts. I was excited to learn she had done a mock spreadsheet on St. Ain's financial situation. It was mock because, of course, it had to be taken from whatever tidbits she'd heard and there had to be a certain amount of conjecture and extrapolation. It was a damn good start though.

Above all, Cora's spreadsheet told a story of a shaky financial picture that significantly improved at just about the time we conjectured that Ron and he had formed an unholy alliance. Corey St. Ain may have just met his match in the women of Marcel.

As Cal and I chose our seat in Scooter's, we enjoyed a little small talk.

"How's Jane doing with her girls?" I asked.

"Oh you know, she runs around like a crazy woman trying to help them with the kids and the homemaking. Without her, it would be so much harder for them to hold careers outside the home. And my poor Jane has her own part-time nursing job to handle. On top of all that, I suppose I'm pretty demanding myself. Did she ask you to have this conversation with me, Donna?"

I laughed. Cal and Jane had married later in life. They each had three grown children from their first spouses, both of whom were deceased. That was a lot of blended family responsibility for both of them. I always marveled at how they kept up with the chaos.

"No Cal, this is strictly about the investment group and Corey St. Ain," I assured him.

He looked a tad sheepish.

"Sorry Donna, guess I just got a little paranoid there for a second. I would hate to think I'm not the husband Jane deserves. I'm so lucky to have found her."

I was happy my friends were so deeply committed to each other. That was another thing I loved about living in the Heartland. Back east, you never heard mention of a spouse without an accompanying complaint. It was not cool to love and respect your spouse back east. It was only cool to bitch and whine – and most everyone did.

"It's fine, Cal, let's just get down to the business at hand."

Almost instantly, Cal switched to an all-business persona. It was impressive. I guess all those years in the operating room required him to focus within split seconds.

We reviewed everything Cal knew about St. Ain and his history. His time with Camerotti and his time in the investment group. Of course, Cal was quick to point out that he rarely ever saw St. Ain, he generally Skyped in on their investor meetings. Cal had a vague notion of about when St. Ain partnered with Ron. He also had a sense that it had gone on for months before he and the other investors became aware. In retrospect, it seemed odd that St. Ain wouldn't be completely open about his joint venture with Ron, since Ron was such an ingrained fixture in the wine industry.

After about 40 minutes of details on St. Ain, some of which were completely new to me, Cal suggested I speak to one of the other investors, Dennis Gamblin. He explained that Gamblin was the investor who seemed to have the closest connection to St. Ain. He was somewhat embarrassed to admit the group thought these two had been drawn together because they were the only two who did not hold a professional or ownership position in a company. And as un PC as that was, they may have been right.

Cal went on to elaborate that Gamblin was an Omaha guy who did some odd jobs around the city. He got connected to the wine industry because of some wine cellars he'd helped to install. A bright guy, Gamblin installed his last two wine cellars in houses of guys in the investment group. He was excited at the prospect of earning some serious coin in an industry about which he was already becoming passionate.

Gamblin lived in a rundown cabin on the outskirts of the city. He had a clear view of the Missouri River and the power plant. The closest he came to being a business owner was the fact that he collected many of the leftovers from his construction jobs. He had them laying around his cabin, both inside and out. Some folks referred to his land as a junkyard, others claimed it was an antique shop of sorts. Either way, Cal suggested taking shots before venturing onto his land. Not to mention that he was armed with a bloodhound and a shotgun, just in case.

Back at the office I decided that Peg, Babs, Cora and I needed another road trip, but I would call Gamblin first. I didn't want to be on the business end of the bloodhound or the shotgun.

It took me a bit to locate his phone number but I finally managed.

"Hello, Mr. Gamblin," I started, "my colleagues and I would like to pay you a visit at noon, to ask you a few questions about your investor group."

"And just why do you suppose I'd want to answer any of your questions?"

"Well, Cal Feisty is a good friend of mine..."

"Why didn't you say so in the first place? If Dr. Feisty sent you over to me, I would be only too glad to help you out."

"That's terrific, Mr. Gamblin, we'll be there about noon."

I rounded up the crew and we headed over to Mr. Gamblin's property on the Missouri. Upon arrival I laughed to myself that I'd even been mildly concerned about the greeting from his bloodhound. Based on his reaction when he approached, it was as though we were ghosts he couldn't see or hear. The four of us greeted Mr. Gamblin and made our introductions as we began to gaze around the property and take in the full extent of the little empire he had built.

His cabin was more like a shack. It appeared as though a half-assed wind would knock it all the way into the river.

And speaking of the river, it wouldn't have far to go as his ramshackle cabin was situated on the downslope of a hill about 10 feet from an amateurish loading dock. It occurred to me that if he slept with his head on the upside of the cabin, he'd never had to worry about reflux. And I was pretty sure no one could eat soup in his cabin without wearing the bulk of it.

As my eyes wandered around the rest of his compact property, I saw a combination of neat and tidy building materials, some quite old and some brand new, as well as a plethora of odd creations. I had to guess he did a lot of work for wealthy folk who got tired of their artistic "finds" and dumped them during the next phase of needless construction. It made for an extremely odd vista, kind of like the Property Brothers meet Willy Wonka. I had to admit it kind of grew on me.

To look at his residence one would surmise that Mr. Gamblin didn't have two nickels to rub together, but one would be wrong. Based on an analysis of his financial holdings, care of Cora, the guy wasn't doing too badly in the money department. Granted, he wasn't loaded like some of his wine cellar clients, but he was far better off than the average middle class guy.

"So now what can I do for you ladies?"

"We're helping the police look into the recent murders of Ed Von Hapsburg and Tim Iremont and we'd like to ask you some questions related to your wine investment group."

"What you really mean to say is that you're snooping and interfering with the police investigation and you're going around bugging anyone related to the case to satisfy your nosiness."

Was it me or was this guy a jerk? My hackles were up and I was going in hot. That's when Peg stepped in.

"Think what you will, sir, but our colleague here, Donna Leigh, has already solved two murders for the police, and they are quick to bring her into any difficult-to-solve investigation."

"Is that so, little lady?" Gamblin smirked.

"I assure you it is most definitely so, and I rarely respond to anyone calling me little lady."

Although a little lady is what she was in actual fact, right now she was a diminutive force to be reckoned with, and I could tell Gamblin got the message since he took a few steps back. I had to admit it was entertaining to watch as level-headed Peg expertly handed this guy his ass. He was not expecting that. And lucky for me, it softened his whole demeanor and made him more amenable to my questions.

After covering much of the same old ground, the stuff we already knew about St. Ain, we finally started to cover some new territory.

"I've never been one to gossip about anyone, especially my investing colleagues," he started, "but I can see that you ladies are doing much more than just sniffing around for gossip. You are on a genuine mission to help our fine police force, and I would never be one to impede justice."

Now we were really getting somewhere. He'd gone from thinking we were a foursome of tottering old Miss Marples to believing we were a special forces unit with OPD. God bless Peg!

I plowed on with my questions, and I think, finally struck a nerve.

"Corey and I were closer than the other investors because we were both outsiders. We were neither of us seriously rich, we both had to scratch and claw for every dime. I knew Corey had a big chip on his shoulder. Those rich bastards took so much for granted and he always felt he had to bow and scrape to them. He really hated that Camerotti guy, although I think I was the only one who knew how he really felt. If you saw him with Camerotti it would make you sick. He would bow and scrape and grovel all day long. And to tell you the truth, I never really thought Camerotti expected it – or even liked it. He seemed to just about tolerate Corey's ass kissing."

That was most interesting, I urged Gamblin to continue.

"Well, things were okay until that Ron guy started doing his best to convince Corey to join his little venture. That's when I told Corey I wanted no more part of any of his doings. I'm a straight arrow and I'm not about to do anything that would convince folks otherwise."

"You are a wise man, Mr. Gamblin." I offered.

"Thanks Ma'am, I like to think so. Anyway, I knew enough to know that Ron was up to no good and I tried to warn Corey a few times, but he was in too deep. I knew when

Mr. Von Hapsburg started snooping around that Corey got real nervous, and with good reason. I think Corey was basically a good guy who just met up with the wrong sort. He thought he'd found a way to make all those rich guys, and especially Mr. Camerotti, pay a price without even realizing it. But what he never realized was that those rich guys got that way for a reason – they're not stupid. I knew it would catch up with him eventually, but I don't think Corey ever really did. The last time I talked to him, he was in a flat out panic."

"And do you recall when that was?" Cora interjected.

"Well now, I think it was less than a week before the Von Hapsburg murder. But I know Corey couldn't have done it."

"And how do you know that?" I asked.

"Well, I know for a fact that he was in California helping Camerotti with his new varietal for the better part of that whole month."

"Isn't it possible that he could have made a quick trip to Omaha to take care of business?" Babs asked.

"No."

"And how can you be so sure of that?" Peg chimed in.

"Because the police checked the flight records and Corey wasn't on any of them. He would never have been able to slip away to drive all that way, so flying would have been the only way, and he didn't fly."

Damn, there it was again. The spotlight shone so clearly on St. Ain, and yet, it couldn't have been him. This was so disappointing. I think we were all feeling the same sense of letdown. We had all been so sure we'd uncover a secret trip out, but what we proved was that a trip would not have been possible. My instincts told me we were so close – and yet.

As I ruminated on my disappointment, I had failed to notice that Peg and Babs had moved closer to the river edge to play with a seemingly barely conscious bloodhound who was lying directly in front of a large and unwieldy modern art sculpture that sat on a narrow base, spreading out and up. It stood about 7 feet tall and was, at its highest point, about 9 feet in circumference. It was a miracle that thing managed to stand upright being on such an extreme slope.

The dog was enjoying getting his belly rubbed and his ears scratched, and he was proving a much needed distraction for my deflated team members. As we were about to wrap the whole session up and head on back to the office, Peg had an inspired thought. It was so inspired that it caused her to jerk up her head and bellow her excitement.

Unfortunately, her violent outburst startled the poor bloodhound out of his wits. He jumped up, smacking soundly into the aforementioned sculpture. Said sculpture teetered for a moment and then lost its balance. It rolled end over end toward the waters of the Missouri. In a panic, Peg, Babs and a wide-awake bloodhound weren't far behind.

Initially, all three came close to catching the runaway sculpture, but it continued to pick up speed as it headed toward the river. One brief hesitation as the sculpture hit a divot in the bank enabled Peg and Babs to grab onto it just as it made its final plunge into the murky waters of the Missouri. And as those of us who took physics know, their strength was no match for the inertia of the moving artwork. All three tumbled unceremoniously into the rapidly moving Missouri, followed by a highly invested bloodhound.

Cora and I both let out a howl and ran to the edge of the bank. On the way, we each grabbed a utensil, she a nearby plank and I a tree branch. When we reached the edge, we ran along the current and offered our respective rescue equipment to the fast traveling women. Eventually, they let go of the sculpture and grabbed onto our plank and branch. We dragged them out of the roiling water as we watched the last of the modern sculpture wend its way down the river and around the bend out of site. The bloodhound, having lost interest, had dog paddled his way to shore and was vigorously shaking off the rivulets of muddy water coating his entire body.

"That there's a shame, ladies," said a chuckling Gamblin, "that statue's gonna cost ya about a hundred bucks."

We looked at each other in horror. Not at all concerned about Mr Gamblin's price tag, we realized the chaos that could ensue in the river if that floating catastrophe wasn't stopped.

After we settled up with Gamblin, we hurried back to the office, some of us sitting atop thick plastics bags for the short ride. We had to research the best means of retrieving our recent purchase in order to keep boaters and swimmers safe from excess and potentially damaging debris. After much Googling, we found a guy who agreed to take his boat out and retrieve the sculpture for us – that would cost us another $200. But it was well worth it. For all we knew, littering into the Missouri could be a serious offense – with jail time.

Unfortunately, Peg never did get to reveal her brilliant thought.

[CHAPTER 29]

$300 poorer and not all that much wiser, Cora, Peg, Babs and I stood outside of the Marcel offices and admired our new company sculpture. It was underwhelming. At least we had done our responsible civic duty and retrieved the carnage from the waters of the Missouri. Liv and Maxie came running out to see what all the fuss was about. Thank goodness Donny was no longer a presence in the office, I couldn't bear to think of what he would have put us through after this latest escapade. My mind flashed back on all of his snarky superiority over the least little thing. This was hardly a little thing.

"I kind of like it," Liv pronounced.

"It's swamp water refuge," Maxie kindly pointed out.

"No, I think I remember when it was on display at a local art gallery, the one on Jackson Street. If I recall, this thing went for a hefty sum back 5 or 6 years ago. I think you guys got us a great find for $300.

And it will look perfect in our front entranceway," Liv proclaimed.

With that declaration, our traveling sculpture had found a new home. Much to my surprise, instead of being tortured and chastised until the end of time, we were given props for getting the deal of a lifetime. This time I didn't try to stop Babs and Peg from looking triumphant. They had earned it. They had both risked their lives to try and save that artwork, and I think Babs still had a rash of unknown origin as proof. No, this time they had earned their praise, and I was not going to deprive them of one second of it.

Where I did get chastised was after briefing Liv and Maxie on our conversation with Gamblin.

"Why would you even bother to go there after we told you that St. Ain could not possibly have committed this crime?" Liv started.

"Yeah Donna, we covered that ground days ago, why did you waste all that time and effort?" Maxie demanded.

For a brief moment I longed for Donny's laughter. I could handle being the butt of his humor far more than feeling the wrath of these two no-nonsense divas. But only for a moment.

I could begrudge them their ire, I knew how I felt when someone doubted my word. Still, I didn't enjoy it.

"Help me out then. Point me in the right direction. For the life of me, my gut tells me St. Ain is the guy."

"We can see why you'd think that." Maxie acknowledged, "We have that same gut feeling, but the facts are the facts."

"Yes, the facts are the facts, but are there other facts that could potentially alter the facts that we know?"

"I'm confused." Liv said.

"So am I." Maxie concurred.

"What she means is, we know that St. Ain was in California,

but was Ron? Or someone else who might have been working with Ron or St. Ain?" Cora explained.

"Ron, you're right. In all the turmoil about St. Ain, we've pretty much left Ron without so much as a by your leave. Maybe now is the time to put Ron under a microscope," Liv concluded.

We stood outside the Marcel doors and discussed our plan for running Ron to ground. This was really enervating. The game was afoot all over again. We split Ron up by the vineyards with which he worked. Maxie and Liv took the Napa vineyards and Cora and I took the Sonoma ones. We each agreed to our marching orders and agreed to review our progress at lunch the next day. I really didn't think I could get pumped up about this investigation all over again, so sure I had totally run out of steam on this one. Thank goodness the team was all raring to go; there was still a lot of legwork to do in order to bring Ed's murderer to justice. I knew I could never have done it alone.

At the end of the day, I was anxious to get home to Jon and the bulldogs. Over a glass of Kim Crawford and a lovely dish of Jon's mushroom risotto, we discussed the events of the day. Apparently, Jon was already apprised of much of the action, because the local news had featured the latest in rafting down the Missouri – on a sculpture. That took some of the wind out of my sails. And the rest was deflated when I related our proposed action steps to Jon.

"No, Ron's not your guy."

"I know you think that, but you can't possibly know that."

"I do know that, and I hate to see you and the team waste any more of your valuable time on a wild goose chase."

I did not expect that. I wasn't sure what to do next. Should I leave Liv and Maxie to their investigation, knowing they were barking up the wrong tree? I mean, Liv had known Jon for years and she had come to respect his instincts on most things. But this was asking for a huge leap of faith.

After much consternation I decided I'd shoot Liv a message suggesting they take things much slower than planned. I shared Jon's comments and qualified that they weren't even remotely scientific. Liv must have been working because a reply was almost instantaneous. It read: If Jon feels that way, there's no way I'm wasting more time on this clown. Let's talk tomorrow about how Jon thinks we should proceed.

Her note left me with mixed feelings. I was glad to have kept Maxie and Liv from spinning their wheels more than necessary, but I had to admit to being a tad resentful of how quick Liv was to adopt Jon's suggestion. Had that thought come from me, I would likely have spent hours defending myself. After berating myself for being a baby, I resolved to focus on the good I had done. Then another thought occurred to me. While I knew what Jon thought we shouldn't focus on, I wasn't clear where he thought our next action steps would be of most benefit. So I asked him.

"Didn't you hypothesize that St. Ain had an accomplice at some point?" he offered.

"I did, but that just felt too much like a 'made for tv' movie."

"I think you should reconsider that possibility."

"But wouldn't Ron..."

"Ron's an idiot."

"An idiot who has a lot of people jumping through hoops because of all his larcenous extra-curricular activities."

"True, but just think about how fast everyone was onto him."

He had a point. Ron was smart enough to think of some crooked schemes, but he wasn't smart enough to pull any of them off for long without being detected. Of course, stupid people murder every day, so that was no alibi for Ron in my book. As I was about to argue this point, Jon beat me to the punch.

"Ron's not your guy."

I was getting sick of this blind faith shit.

"And you know that?" I asked.

"I know that. First of all, Ron isn't in Omaha very often himself, but his whereabouts could certainly be checked easily enough. My sense is that if Ron had committed these murders, he would have been detected within the first few hours. Our murderer was much smarter than Ron."

"Any ideas on who we should be watching?"

"Some, but none I'm ready to share with you at this point."

"So you know who the killer is?"

"What I've already written down hasn't changed."

"So let me ask you just a few more questions."

"Shoot."

"You believe that St. Ain was the person in charge of the murders, and that he had an accomplice in Omaha who actually did the deed?"

"Correct."

"Is it anyone we know?"

"I think so."

"Someone we know well?"

"I'd rather not say more."

Thus ended our tranquil evening at home. Was I feeling tranquil? You tell me!

* * *

The next day was expected to be a bear. We were all flat out, Liv with a string of meetings, Maxie who would be spending the day strategizing with our largest client, Cora closing out the prior month's books, and I scouting out some venues for a client's major event. Knowing how the day was shaping up, we'd all agreed to my suggestion that we start an hour early and meet for coffee at Aroma's. It would be our only chance to create a game plan for moving forward.

"Donna, why don't you call Cal again? See if he has any thoughts on this mysterious Omaha connection," suggested Cora.

I agreed reluctantly I really didn't think there was anything more that Cal could tell me. But it was worth a shot.

"I will recontact Gamblin and press him for people St. Ain would have known in Omaha," continued Cora.

I thought this would also be a dead end, but Cora was on a roll – who was I to stop her?

"Maxie and Liv, you hold tight until we get the results from these calls, then maybe we'll have some more names to run down."

"That's fine with me," Liv agreed, "I have no time for anything murder-related today anyway."

"I'm kind of glad that Jon steered us off of Ron anyway," Maxie admitted, "I think someone that crooked and that dumb could be seriously dangerous. I'd just as soon avoid him like the plague."

We all agreed to Cora's plan, as well as the fact that we would have to share any findings in email if they materialized later today. We would never get a chance to get the four of us in a room again until tomorrow at the earliest.

As expected, our day was pandemonium, I never even saw the other three throughout the rest of the day. At about 2 pm I realized that any call I wanted to have with Cal would have to wait until tonight.

As it turned out, I never did make that call to Cal.

[CHAPTER 30]

Warren left me a message to "stop in" to the station on my way home. Her tone was so ominous. In my two prior murder investigations, I don't think I ever received a similar message from her, and my Jersey paranoia was kicking in, in full gear. By the end of the day, I was a virtual bundle of nerves.

I arrived at the station and the desk clerk whisked me into Warren's office. She wasted no time in sharing her news.

"Donna, I'm going to tell you something that's a bit shocking."

This did nothing to calm the nerves.

"Ed is alive."

I waited.

"I said Ed is alive."

"I know what you said, but what does that mean?"

"We faked his death."

I've never had vertigo before, but I was pretty sure I was experiencing my first episode. Warren's desk was on the ceiling and her wall unit was flat on the floor, where I expected to join it at any moment.

"What? Why? So there was never an accident or a fatality?"

"No, there was," she replied.

"We knew that Ed was in danger from some of the investigating he'd been doing for associates in the wine business. Some of the folks he was poking around did not like to be poked."

Now that was really puzzling. I pressed for details and Warren explained that a car resembling that of Ed's had been parked in a spot frequented by Ed. The killer assumed it was Ed's car and tampered with the brakes. When the police realized the extent of the danger, they located Ed and whisked him away to a hiding place that even Eva and Abby did not know about at first.

I started to get an odd sensation. So many thoughts were circling through my brain, none of them had quite made it to my mouth in any kind of an intelligible fashion. I let Warren continue.

"Eva and Abby have known since before Ed's memorial. They felt terrible going through with it and seeing you all suffer so, but we insisted that they play along since it was the only foolproof way of keeping Ed safe.

"But the papers in the dump..."

"Planted to throw off the killer."

"And Tim?"

"Tim was not as fortunate as Ed. We didn't think he would be in the same kind of danger. That was a costly miscalculation. When the killer found a key in with the papers he stole, he naturally assumed more evidence would be secreted in the warehouse, so he went back. Tim was just collateral damage."

On a slightly more upbeat note, Warren went on to elaborate.

"And Ed is one of those rare, lucky fellows who got to experience the outpouring of love that was meant to be post mortem."

"How?"

"He watched his whole memorial through closed circuit TV, and thoroughly enjoyed the Hungarian menu with the specially selected wines. In fact, we sneaked him an abundance of both so he got to eat his own funeral dinner. Actually, his only comment was that he would have preferred to bake the desserts himself, but under the circumstances they were certainly edible."

My mind immediately jumped to my sappy and weepy behavior at Ed's fake memorial. Oh crap! I was sure to take some shit over that. If there had been one good thing about Ed's passing it was that he wouldn't be around to mock my indulgent, perhaps even excessive, grief over his death.

As I neared home after meeting with Warren it occurred to me, the shock of Ed's reincarnation had rendered my brain virtually useless. I had completely forgotten to ask about the identity of the killer. I could only assume they had him/her in custody or they would not have begun to release the news of Ed's miraculous recovery.

* * *

Our "Welcome Back Ed" party was a huge extravaganza leaving his memorial in the dust. We partied like there'd be no tomorrow – and put a major dent in the remaining stock from Ed's warehouse. As expected, I took a rash of shit from Ed on the uncharacteristic display of my "softer side" during the days and weeks after his death was announced. But then, I was able to ride him about having to supply the booze at his own 'back to the living' bash.

"Wow, Donna, thank god I'm still here now that the world knows you couldn't go on without me," Ed cooed in an annoying fashion. "And good luck trying to deny it now."

"Don't flatter yourself, Big Foot," I replied. "I value life, even worthless, waste of a good pair of chinos life like yours."

And this went on, in intervals, for the bulk of the evening. At one point I found myself wishing for a break cutting tool myself – but of course, I'd never want to hurt Ed's family.

Once the bulk of the bullshit was out of the way, I had a chance to really talk to both Ed and Eva. They expressed their sincere appreciation for everything I did, along with everyone else who helped in an attempt to bring Ed's perceived killer to justice.

As I looked around the room, I could see the whole crowd partying their little hearts out. This kind of a wake-up call is the best kind of incentive to shake things up in your life – and I was definitely seeing a little shaking going on in front of me.

"Hey Ed, I'm hoping your return will help Nic get back to himself. He's been so out of sorts these past several weeks."

As soon as I'd uttered this last statement, Ed and Eva both exhibited the strangest looks on their faces.

"What? Did I say something?"

"Don't you know?"

"Apparently not, know what?"

"Donna," Jon interjected, "Nic is the murderer, didn't Warren tell you?"

"What? No. That can't be right. Not Nic, Le Voltaire Nic? He's not the murderer!"

"He is. And he has bolted," Ed added.

"I don't understand. Why didn't Warren tell me? How do you know this?"

"Well, Donna, I'm guessing she felt you'd had enough shock just learning I was still alive. Clearly, Warren knew that learning Nic was the killer would be a major shock to you as well. And that's not all. Nic didn't try to kill me because of personal reasons, Nic was a killer for hire."

"Now I know you're just kidding, Ed. You really had me going there."

"Sorry Donna, this is no joke. Nic had been a killer for hire, based in Omaha for the past six years. He took a job as a waiter for Olivier as a cover. The police have tied him back to over 150 murders between Grand Island and Des Moines over the past 6 years. The list is impressive. For a time, he did a lot of the really dirty work for a large PR firm called NED. Those guys thought they were Robin Hood. They did a lot of good, but it's just now starting to come out that they also did a whole lot of horrible."

I had to sit down. This wasn't really happening. Nic was my friend. Nic bought toys and treats for my dogs, Nic made me special drinks on special occasions.

"I know what you're thinking. Nic was an awesome guy. But his main job was to be a paid killer, and that took precedent over everything."

"So who paid him to kill you?"

"That was St. Ain."

"I knew it!"

"Apparently, St. Ain would have done anything to really fit in at Camerotti and in the investor group. He was always just a square peg in a round hole in constant search of a way to prove himself to no avail. The day came when he finally gave up. That's when that sleazeball Ron came along and used St. Ain to further his little skimming deal. Ron also convinced St. Ain to play fast and loose with some of the investor money. In St. Ain's eyes, he saw me ruining several things for him. I was onto Ron and would likely have taken St. Ain down with him. And I was also creating heat in the investor group – St. Ain could ill afford that either. So he decided he had to have me killed. And then, of course, poor Tim when St. Ain sent Nic in search of some of the damning papers."

"Unbelievable."

"St. Ain will go to jail for a very long time, and as for Ron, the west coast Bartonis have taken him into the fold.

He has a long future of being their riddler."

"What?"

"You know, the riddler," Jon replied, "the guy who turns the champagne bottles periodically when they're stored in the wall."

"A riddler, but do they still..."

"They believe a lifetime of nothing else will be fitting punishment for their errant relative," Ed jumped in. I can't imagine the life of boredom, not to mention poverty that's in store for Ron. Look, I know this has to be difficult for you to assimilate what with everything else. It must all seem very surreal. But at least you should have a great feeling of pride."

"Why?"

"Well, Warren tells me that without your detective work they would not have pinpointed Nic when they did. She said you had voiced some concerns about his behavior, and then they were able to tie that physical lead directly back to his handwriting. Yes, according to Warren, you practically, single-handedly solved this case."

I don't know what was more of a shock, that Nic was a contract killer, or that I had saved the day and solved the case for the police. This would not be a day I would soon forget.

In all the commotion surrounding Ed's official rise from the dead, I had completely forgotten to ask about the real victim of Ed's intended killer. I scanned the room and found my target, Warren had stopped in for a toast as she'd promised. Once at her side, I blurted at least a dozen questions within the course of about fifteen seconds. Before she responded, I noticed a curious expression on Warren's face. It was an odd blend of sympathy (for me?) and authority. Very puzzling.

"Donna, I'm sorry to have to tell you this," she began.

That was really puzzling. I pressed for details and Warren again explained that a car resembling that of Ed's had been parked in a spot frequented by Ed. Nic assumed it was Ed's car and tampered with the brakes. When the police realized the extent of the danger, they located Ed and whisked him away to a hiding place. Even Eva and Abby did not know about the deception at first.

I started to get an odd sensation.

"So who was killed in the car?"

"It was Donny."

[EPILOGUE]

The next day I entered the office with some trepidation, but my concerns were unwarranted. Everything was exactly as normal. For a moment I wondered if they'd heard about Donny yet – but with our crew and their connection to social media – they knew. And still nothing.

I thought back to the day we'd all found out about Ed. The difference was tremendous. I guess not everyone leaves a swath of sorrow in their wake. You really do learn something new every day.

Naturally, I wouldn't be satisfied until I knew the circumstances surrounding Donny's demise. I mean, even if I wasn't exactly broken-hearted, I was still curious. In all the commotion surrounding Ed's rising from the dead, I had completely forgotten about the real victim of Ed's intended killer. I knew the basics of how they faked Ed's death from our conversation at Ed's "back to life" party, but I needed to know more, so I called her.

"It's simple, and sad," Warren warned. "Donny had a car very similar to Ed's. On that particular day he happened to be running errands and he chose a parking spot that Ed often frequented. Nic thought it was Ed's car."

"You mean Donny was killed because he was in the wrong place at the wrong time? A victim of circumstance?"

"That's about it."

In all the years I knew Donny, through all his bark and bluster, I knew the one thing he would hate about this was the fact that he was insignificant in his own death.

The End

ABOUT THE AUTHOR

Robin Donovan is the author of the blog, Menologues, a humorous yet informative look at the trials and tribulations of menopause by someone who's been there. Menologues is republished on two commercial sites: Vibrant Nation and Alltop, and has won regional honors for social media at the AMA Pinnacles and PRSA Paper Anvil awards.

Donovan was born and raised in New Jersey but lived and worked in Connecticut for a number of years before moving to Nebraska in 1999. Starting her career as a high school English teacher, Donovan moved into advertising in the early 80's. In 1999 she accepted a job offer from Bozell, an Omaha based ad agency. In late 2001, she and three colleagues purchased Bozell from its New York based parent company.

Donovan lives with her husband and three bulldogs, Roxi, Sadie (Sweet Pea) and Frank.

The following is an excerpt from the second book
in the Donna Leigh Mysteries Series,

I Didn't Kill Her

But That May Have Been Shortsighted

I DIDN'T KILL HER

BUT THAT MAY HAVE BEEN SHORTSIGHTED

A DONNA LEIGH MYSTERY BY ROBIN LEEMANN DONOVAN

(2nd in a series of Donna Leigh Mysteries)

[CHAPTER 1]

It was Wednesday and I was running a bit late. I ran across the south parking lot with purse and tote bag in one hand and 12-pack of Diet Orange Sunkist in the other. Burdened with an unwieldy load, I moved precariously through both the front door and the outer lobby entrance. Once inside I wound my way around the tall wooden, teepee-like structures that served both as organic art installations and intimate meeting pods and veered past rows of sleek wood and black laminate desk units carefully balancing my parcels. Upon reaching my desk, I dumped the load and logged on to my computer. The meeting reminder popped up with a 'bing' to confirm a 10:00 A.M. conference call, reminding me to reread the project file before jumping on the call.

I noticed my message light blinking and hoped it would

be something quick. I'd have to hustle if I was going to review that file. The message was from Ken Farley. It had been years since I'd given Ken a thought. He and I had worked together at an ad agency in southern Connecticut for a number of years, which now seemed like a lifetime ago. The message was oddly cryptic.

"Wow Donna, that must have been some shock for you, huh? All things considered, you must be really torn about how to feel. I'd sure love to know what you're thinking."

I couldn't imagine what on earth he could be talking about.

Oh well, no point in taxing my brain. I might as well just call him. Logic would dictate that I wait until AFTER the conference call to indulge my curiosity, but I'd never been a slave to logic.

Once on the phone, Ken was no less cryptic. I put up with about two minutes of his nonstop gibberish before I started to lose my temper.

"Hey Ken, what the hell are you talking about?!"

My impatience seemed to help him focus.

"You mean you haven't heard?" he asked.

"Guess not." I tried to hide my annoyance. "Why don't you fill me in?"

"Your old buddy Betty Jean bought the farm!"

"Thornton?"

"That's what I'm saying," Ken pressed, "you didn't hear about it?"

"How would I have heard about it all the way out here in Omaha?" He really could be thick sometimes.

"Man, Donna, You're not saying you didn't know she moved to Omaha three months ago?"

The man was talking pure nonsense now. Betty Jean and I had worked together for several years when I was in Connecticut. After my move to Omaha ten years earlier I had seen neither hide nor hair of BJ. In fact, it had probably been another two years prior to that. Not seeing BJ was definitely how I liked it. The thought of her moving to the Heartland? I would never buy that! She fancied herself a big city "player" and a fashionista. There was no way she was moving to Omaha, Nebraska.

I harbor no such fancies. Having lived my whole life as an Easterner, I virtually leapt at the opportunity to join the prestigious advertising firm, Marcel, when the call came from an overzealous recruiter. Once I knew it was Marcel there was no looking back. If that meant a move to Omaha – so be it! At the time, I had no way of knowing that public holding company shell games would result in my opportunity to buy the very advertising brand I had respected from afar for so many years. Now, my partners and I were charged with the sacred task of taking this revered icon of communication into the next phase of marketing.

BJ's self-delusion did not stop at her perceived importance in the world of business. She also considered herself to be fashion-forward in the extreme. She was right about extreme. On the fashion side of the equation, she and I could not have been more different. Tailored black business was my wardrobe staple. Admittedly it wasn't exactly ground-breaking, but at least I'd never arrived at a business dinner attired in a white linen jumpsuit, festooned from neck to toe with twelve-inch tall basketball players as had my former nemesis, Betty Jean. In my humble opinion, she could not have looked more ridiculous if she'd been wearing the 50-gallon garbage drum parked by the side door. Yet she faced a sea of Brooks Brothers clad marketers with a smug, almost arrogant, smile on her self-satisfied face. She perused the room to ensure that everyone had taken notice of her latest fashion statement. A lingering glance must have sated her obsessive desire for attention; there was no denying that every eye in the room rested on her. That was one amazing thing about BJ. She lacked the ability to discern a difference between genuine admiration, as *rarely as that occurred*, from a thinly veiled attempt to keep from laughing in her face. It was that blissful ignorance which enabled her to bask in delusions of imagined grandeur as she stood there in her outrageous garb and preened. I almost envied her that.

Now Ken was saying BJ is dead? It just wasn't sinking in. This had to be some kind of a lame joke. It was hard enough to accept that she was dead much less that she had died in, of all places, Omaha, Nebraska, my home.

The following is an excerpt from the first book
in the Donna Leigh Mysteries Series,

**Is It Still Murder
Even If She Was A Bitch?**

IS IT STILL MURDER
EVEN IF SHE WAS A BITCH?

A DONNA LEIGH MYSTERY BY ROBIN LEEMANN DONOVAN

(1st in a series of Donna Leigh Mysteries)

[CHAPTER 1]

Claire Dockens was dead. Wow, that was a shock. When Kyle told me I almost dropped right on the spot. How often is it that someone you've known for years, worked with in the trenches, whose house you've been to several times, drops dead? She wasn't even that old – like early fifties.

If that weren't enough of a bombshell, Kyle's next revelation definitely put me over the edge – "And they say she was murdered." At that point I think I did lose consciousness for a second or two – not enough to make me actually hit the floor – but I'm sure, moments later, I wasn't facing in exactly the same direction as I had been before my momentary lapse.

The next thought that entered my shock-addled head was, "I wonder if they'll suspect me? I mean, it's not like I could stand her."

Then, Kyle said, "Gosh, I hope they won't think I did it."

Kyle Thoroughgood was my colleague and friend at Marcel, the oldest and most revered advertising and marketing consulting firm in Omaha, Nebraska. We'd both been colleagues of the victim a few years prior, and the day that Claire tendered her resignation had been an occasion of mutual celebration. Her mere existence had elicited an intense aggravation in both Kyle and me. She'd openly sought to condemn and abuse us for her own personal sport. With Claire as a colleague, we definitely hadn't needed any enemies. Truthfully, Kyle and I were but two of her multitude of victims since verbally abusive banter was her preferred pastime, but with the two of us she'd taken it to a level beyond. She had elevated her abuse to an art form.

That's when we both heaved a sigh of relief. Hell, the list of suspects would be monumentally huge! Sure we'd be on it – but undoubtedly we'd get lost in the shuffle of characters with sufficient motive.

"So how'd they do it?" I tentatively pressed.

"Bludgeoned as she was leaving a charity dinner," Kyle offered.

"Oh god, that really could have been any of us," I shuddered. "With what?"

Still nodding Kyle responded, "Hasn't been released yet. I don't think they're sure. From what I know they haven't found the weapon and the autopsy is scheduled for tomorrow morning."

"Oh yeah, how'd you find out?"

"Facebook."

That's when my partner Liv walked by with her third coffee of the morning. "Gotta run – late for a meeting," she tossed out, and then, "Shit, does coffee come out of silk?" As she frantically swiped at the growing brown stain on her new couture blouse.

"Hey," Kyle pursued "hear about Claire?"

"I read it on Facebook at 2 a.m. last night when I was finishing the proposal for this meeting. Her poor family!"

Leave it to Liv to give the kind, humanitarian response. Liv Danielsen was my partner and fellow owner of Marcel. I'm Donna Leigh. Ten years prior Liv and I had the amazing opportunity to purchase Marcel, the legendary ad agency that had once grown to global status and revenue before being purchased by a somewhat short-sighted holding company and allowed to idle long enough for Liv, two other partners and myself to buy the company. Over the years, our other two partners had eased out and/or retired. Liv and I hand-picked a third partner who had worked with us to reposition the business and shed the "ad agency" persona that was killing every agency unable to make the jump into the future and the world of social media and one-on-one dialogs with customers: Donny Miller.

"Kyle and I are on a mission to identify the murder weapon."

Liv just rolled her eyes and grabbed a damp cloth. She dabbed at her spreading stain while running toward the already packed conference room.

I turned back to Kyle in time to see Donny motoring up the hallway. "I suppose you know about Claire too?"

One thing about Donny; he was connected. If you needed anything you could count on him to hook you up with the best in the city. With his pervasive human network in place it was virtually impossible to be the bearer of any kind of news to Donny, because there was nothing he hadn't already heard.

"Hell yes, two of my high school buddies were cops on the scene. One of them texted me even before the coroner pronounced her dead. I would have run down to check it out — but he didn't think his CO would be too thrilled. I tried you on your cell. Man, this will really be a blow to the Omaha business community. She was unquestionably one of the smart ones, one of the few I could really respect."

"You're kidding."

"Yeah, she didn't know anything." He smiled impishly. "She sure thought she did though. One thing's for sure — they won't have a shortage of suspects. Hey Donna, now that I think of it, you're probably on the list — you too, Kyle."

Now Kyle and I did the eye roll. Typical Donny. But this time he'd kind of struck a nerve. I could tell by the look on Kyle's face that we were thinking the same thing — would we be getting a visit from a detective anytime soon? Exciting as that may have sounded, we didn't want any public notoriety that would give our clients reason to believe that we could not give them our full focus.

That was when it struck Kyle. He excused himself to call the clients and give them a heads up that the murder victim was one of our former employees. Poor guy, he'd be stuck ducking tough questions while short on information, and forced to appear respectfully sad and inordinately complimentary to a person who made his life hell every chance she got. But that's the way it goes – once a team member always a team member, and even though Claire hadn't been a member of the Marcel team at the time of her death – he wasn't about to speak ill of the dead. Actually, Kyle never speaks ill of anyone. Fortunately for me I can sometimes make him laugh with my blunt and irreverent characterizations of some of our well-deserving colleagues and associates. I'm not as nice as Kyle.

I rolled my eyes at Donny and headed back toward my office passing two puzzled-looking copywriters. One thing was for certain, it would be a while before we lacked a topic of conversation.

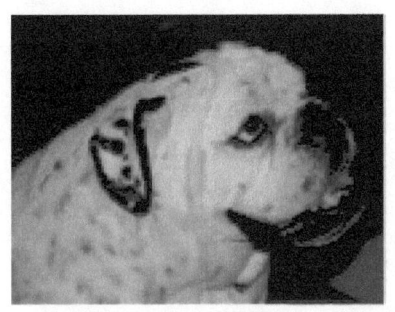

Gracie Dancer LLC

www.rldonovan.com